Taken by Storm

~ A Novella ~

& Other Short Stories

Taken by Storm

~ A Novella ~

& Other Short Stories

Blake Channels

Blossom Cove Publishing

Taken by Storm & Other Short Stories. Copyright © 2020 by Blake Channels.

Cover art by stock_colors.
Cover design by J. Brown.

Published by Blossom Cove Publishing.

To find out more about the author and available books, visit blakechannels.com.

For Iris –

A dear friend and mentor who encouraged me not to be the old lady who died with a stack of unpublished books beneath her bed.

Contents

Taken by Storm

Marigold Summer

Where Hearts Are Mended

Taken by Storm

CHAPTER ONE

*A*bigail Travis closed her vivid green eyes and tried to picture the perfect day. The glowing sun would be rising over the majestic blue water, coloring the skies in brilliant hues of yellow and orange. She would sip her chai tea latte while gazing lazily out at the view from her front porch. She would breathe in the salty, sea air as the wind swept through her honey-blonde hair—completely at peace that there was nowhere she needed to be. Her yellow Lab, Chester, would be curled up at her feet, his tail thumping happily against the wooden deck slats. Her half-read book would rest face down on the patio table, all but forgotten with the emergence of the glorious sunrise. Yes, that would be the perfect day.

Today would not be one of those days. Besides the obvious—she had neither a dog, nor a view of the water (not to mention she was on the wrong coastline if she wanted to catch the sun rising over the ocean). But in addition to these inconvenient realities, she also had an unexpected meeting with her boss that she wasn't looking forward to. The corners of her full mouth turned down into a frown as she reread that morning's text message for the umpteenth time. She sighed, then slipped her cellphone back into her purse and reached for her car keys on the nightstand. After shoving her keys into the right pocket of her jeans, she glanced around the bedroom for her shoes.

Her manager, Tammie, had texted at the appalling hour of five a.m. The irritating pinging sound had alerted her to the message, ripping her from a sound sleep and thrusting her into a reality her tired body wasn't yet prepared to face. The contents of the text were cryptic, and the message had Abigail stewing for the past hour.

Need to discuss your recent assignment. My office. First thing.

Well, for starters, what was *first thing*? She was used to getting to the office around seven-thirty a.m., but Tammie barely managed to roll in before nine. Was the meeting important enough for her fitness-enthusiast boss to skip her precious morning yoga routine and come in earlier?

Abigail's latest assignment was turning out to be a challenge, to put it delicately. She'd been tasked with keeping Storm Jackson, Hollywood bad-boy and the silver screen's hottest star (opinion of the tabloid magazines and not necessarily her own), out of trouble. As a senior staffer at Caldwell's, a small but prominent PR firm located in the heart of Los Angeles, she was used to being assigned the tough cases; but she worried her current assignment might break her. Storm wasn't her first celebrity client, but he was certainly proving to be her most taxing.

Well-placed *puff pieces* in reputable magazines, guest spots on family-friendly morning shows, intentionally *leaked* photos to the press of Storm volunteering at a soup kitchen—Abigail had pulled out all the stops to redefine his image. But each time she had a win, her client would act out publicly, overshadowing all she had accomplished. One step forward, and two steps back—they were stuck in an absurd line dance. Abigail detested line dancing.

"What kind of name is Storm Jackson anyways?" she grumbled aloud to herself. "See, now you're making me talk to myself like a crazy person," she continued with her morning rant as she rooted around for her sneakers. Finally locating them in the far corner of the room, she sat down on the floor and tugged them on. Her manager probably wouldn't approve of her casual wardrobe choice, but today she was in no mood to please. If she were lucky, Storm would be reassigned. Perhaps to one of the PR staff that bought into his line of crap and his *I'm such a hunk* nonsense.

It wasn't that Abigail didn't find Storm attractive. His rugged good looks were indisputable. Tall, muscular build with a strong jawline. Thick, dark hair. Bold, soulful eyes that were an enchanting blend of cerulean blue and emerald green; eyes she'd had to remind herself more than once not to get lost in. He exuded virility and an irresistible confidence. The problem with Storm Jackson was that he was fully aware of his sex appeal and played on those strengths. A lot.

His infamous charm and flagrant disregard for the rules were the reasons Abigail had him as a client. Dozens of local and national tabloids had Storm's picture splashed across their front covers for the past several months. There were compromising photos of him with various women (supermodels, actresses, and unknown females alike), a mugshot after an arrest for illegal street racing, and a photograph of him involved in an all-out brawl outside of a nightclub in which he'd narrowly escaped another arrest. His motion picture company threatened to release him from his contract, but Storm's agent promised he would get his client's image cleaned up within thirty days, in time for the release of his latest movie, *Higher Caliber 3*.

Abigail suspected the brass at Xander-Kelly Motion Pictures was bluffing. Storm was wildly popular, and his movies were far too successful to release him from his contract, but she kept the suspicion to herself. She didn't want to talk herself out of a job. Then again, the way things were going, perhaps she did.

When she'd first met Storm, he'd tried his seductive charms on her, but she'd made it abundantly clear from the beginning that she wasn't interested. "I haven't seen any of your movies, nor do I agree with your recent *Sexiest Man Alive* status, so let's get that out of the way right now, Mr. Jackson." To his credit, he hadn't retaliated in anger or asked to be assigned to a different PR specialist. He'd just shrugged and moved on to flirting with her assistant instead.

She'd lied, of course. Abigail had seen almost all his movies. Her ex-boyfriend was an action movie buff. And after only a few minutes with him, she was convinced Storm might very well be the sexiest man alive. At least that she'd ever had the fortune of meeting. But it was another speculation she kept to herself.

Before rushing out the door she ran a brush through her shoulder-length hair, swept a bronzing powder across her high cheekbones to apply a subtle, sun-kissed glow one might expect a native Californian to already have, and practiced a courteous smile to mask the annoyance written all over her face.

When she arrived at work, she spotted Tammie's car in the parking lot. "Darn it. I guess 'first thing' meant a little earlier," she muttered under her breath as she got out of her car. She swept a strand of honey-blonde hair off her shoulder, looked down with regret at her tattered sneakers, then headed for her boss's office. She knocked twice, then swung the frosted glass door open without being invited in. She figured her intrusion was no more invasive than Tammie's five a.m. text and hoped her boss would be too surprised by the abrupt entrance to take notice of her unprofessional wardrobe.

Tammie looked up from her desk, a surprised look on her stern face. "Good morning," she said crossly. Abigail shifted her stance uncomfortably, then stepped into the office, closing the door behind her. If she was about to be bawled out, she didn't need witnesses. She took a seat across from Tammie, squaring her shoulders and mentally preparing herself for the dressing down her boss was so gifted at giving.

"You wanted to see me?" She tried to sound chipper. It came out sounding forced and a little high-pitched.

Tammie raised an eyebrow into a sharp point, conveying her disappointment without words. "Yes I did." She slid the latest tabloid across her desk so Abigail had no choice but to read it. She tapped her index finger in the general direction of the words she found so offensive as she made a disapproving clucking sound with her tongue. "Explain, please."

Abigail picked up the paper and tried to keep her face void of emotion as she read the latest headline. *Storming the Castle*, it read in bold print, just above the picture of Storm and an attractive blonde woman entering Tribulation Castle, a museum in downtown Los Angeles known for its erotic art. "So, he enjoys the arts," Abigail said lamely. Visiting an erotic art museum was *hardly* the worst thing her client had done of late and she wondered what had her boss so spun up.

"Don't you recognize who he's with?" Tammie shrieked.

"Should I?"

"That is Judge Masterson's wife!"

Abigail did recognize the name. Judge Masterson was a powerful man and was even rumored to have ties to the mob. Most people were afraid to cross him. "His soon to be *ex-wife* if I'm not mistaken. And she may be married, but at least she's not a prostitute, right?" Abigail wasn't sure why she was defending the situation. Perhaps it was because each immoral decision her client made felt like a personal failure on her part. Plus, if she was being honest, she didn't much care for the judge and was secretly impressed Storm wasn't amongst the masses so afraid of getting on his bad side.

"Well, as far as the studio is concerned, there isn't a distinction. The point is that woman is still married. And to a prominent man in society. A man who could make all our lives difficult if he wanted. This is a blow, Abigail." She once again raised an accusatory eyebrow and pursed her lips in disapproval, but before Abigail could respond, she continued. "Listen, I know this isn't your fault. You can no more control this *actor* than you can control the tide."

Despite her predicament, Abigail smirked at the way her boss enunciated the word *actor*. It was clear she didn't hold the profession in the highest regard. It was also clear she was one of the few women on the planet who didn't find Storm irresistible.

"I have a new idea," Tammie continued. "Mr. Jackson and his agent will be here any minute to discuss it." As if on cue there was a knock on the door. "Come in," she barked. Despite her words of welcome, her tone was anything but inviting.

Storm Jackson stepped into the cramped office with his agent, Harry Burgess, in tow. Wearing an untucked charcoal colored button-up shirt with the top button undone, dark jeans, and leather Oxfords, Storm looked like he'd just stepped out of a magazine. He strode confidently over to the desk, picked up the tabloid and chuckled to himself as he read the headline. His headline. He set the paper back down, still smiling—not even a flicker of shame on his handsome face. Abigail wondered if he was being genuine or if his lack of humility was merely an act.

"Harry, I hope you've explained to your client that this really isn't a laughing matter," Tammie said coldly as if Storm wasn't even in the room.

"Why?" Storm cut in. "Because she's married to some loser judge who doesn't have the decency to relinquish his hold on her and let her out of a loveless marriage?" He didn't sound angry, only matter of fact.

"Storm, you're not helping," Harry warned him. Then, directing his question at Tammie, he asked, "If I'm not mistaken, you have a revised plan?"

Abigail remained silent, equally curious about this new plan. She was fresh out of ideas.

"It has become clear to me, Mr. Jackson, that you need someone with you at all times, to help, um, regulate your decisions."

"Like a human moral compass?" Storm quipped. A glimmer of amusement danced in his beautiful, turquoise eyes.

"Something like that," she answered, unsmiling. "Abigail here will act in that capacity." Abigail opened her mouth to object, but then closed it. Surely her client would object to this preposterous plan, saving her from having to argue with her boss.

"Go on," he said instead, much to the surprise of everyone in the room.

Tammie sighed with impatience. "Abigail's constant presence will raise some questions, so her cover will be that she is your girlfriend."

"My girlfriend, really? And who would believe that?"

"Oh, I'm sorry if I'm not as *amazing* as the platinum blonde, anorexic supermodels you're used to parading around with." Abigail was both surprised and embarrassed at her outburst.

"That's not what I meant." He shot her an apologetic look and appeared uncomfortable for the first time. Turning back to Tammie he said, "I just meant that no one would believe that I would have a steady girlfriend."

"That's what will be perfect about it," Tammie explained, her patience dangling by a thread. She was used to people acting on her requests without comment or objection. "The tabloids will be spinning with how Abigail was able to tame Hollywood's most eligible bachelor.

This will allow her to remain by your side without raising suspicion, which *hopefully* means she can keep you out of trouble."

She shot Storm a warning look before continuing. "The stable relationship will gain you approval points with the studio, and the added positive publicity should boost the film."

Storm rocked back on his heels, rubbing his hand over the stubble on his chin. His intense eyes narrowed in thought.

Abigail looked over at him in exasperation as the heat of humiliation spread across her face. "You're not actually considering this, are you?"

Storm took note of her pleading tone. "Well, would it really be all that bad? You could be my conscience. My own little cricket." He flashed her his brilliant-white, charming smile.

"I'll never be your own little anything," she fumed. She despised herself for letting him get under her skin so easily.

"My own feisty little cricket," he amended, chuckling. Abigail shook her head and took a deep breath. "C'mon," Storm prodded. "It really is a good plan. And the movie comes out in a little over two weeks, so you'll only have to put up with me until then."

Ignoring his comment, Abigail turned to Tammie instead. "But Mr. Jackson isn't my only client," she reminded her.

"Relax, Katerina said she'd be more than happy to handle your other clients for the next couple of weeks. Consider this like a vacation."

Abigail's green eyes flashed with anger. Her boss was keenly aware this wouldn't be a vacation—and she was also aware Katerina was known for poaching other people's clients. Abigail surmised

Tammie was presenting her with a veiled threat–make this work, or risk losing your clientele.

"Fine," Abigail said, conceding defeat. "Two weeks." Then glaring in her boss's direction, she said, "But I'll be needing hazard pay." And with that, she stalked out of the room and headed towards the elevator.

"Wait up," she heard Storm yell from behind her, but she didn't slow down. He picked up his pace until he was at a steady jog. "Hey, what's the rush? Aren't you supposed to stay by my side at all times?" When he caught up with her, he was grinning widely and she had to resist the urge to slug him. "I mean, I think you might already be failing at this assignment," he teased.

Abigail stopped and turned towards him. She took in his handsome face, striking eyes, and crooked grin; reminding herself not to let it distract her from her new responsibilities. "Mr. Jackson, if you wish to remain by my side, I'm afraid you're going to have to learn to keep up." She flashed him her best smile, then sauntered into the elevator.

She was all poise and confidence until they reached the parking garage. Spotting her old, battered car in the far corner of the lot, she stopped mid-stride. Storm was used to hotrods and limo rides. She wondered what he'd make of squeezing into her four-door sedan with the faded red paint and worn, cloth seats. It wasn't that she couldn't afford a nicer car. But she'd had her car since she left home. Her father had helped pick it out. It got her through college, and it saw her through her first job, two failed, semi-serious relationships, and the purchase of her home. And since her car continued to pass its emissions tests each year, she'd found no reason to buy a new one. Until perhaps that very moment.

"What's wrong?" Storm asked.

She shot him an apologetic look. "Um, what did you drive here?"

"Harry and I took a car service. He's probably long gone by now. I have to admit the old goat's getting a little frustrated with me these days."

I can imagine, Abigail thought. "My car may not be, err, what you're used to." For reasons she couldn't fathom, she was stammering and her cheeks flushed. Since when did she care what he thought anyways?

"Cricket, it's fine."

"Cricket? My name is Abigail," she said, not bothering to mask her annoyance. How could he not know her name by now?

"No, you're my personal conscience, remember?" Despite her annoyance, she laughed at his analogy. She led him to her car and manually unlocked the driver's side door before climbing behind the wheel and leaning over to unlock the passenger side door. She plucked a pair of discarded flats from the passenger seat, momentarily considering changing into them and striking a match to her sneakers. She tossed the flats into the backseat instead.

Storm climbed into the passenger side. He moved the seat backwards, giving his long legs some room. "I used to have a car just like this," he told her as he reclined the seat. He inhaled deeply, appreciating the car's faint scent of coconut and vanilla.

"Yeah, right," she laughed.

"I'm serious. My family wasn't wealthy and back then I was a bit reckless. When I got my driver's license my parents told me there was no way they were going to buy me a fancy car only to see me wrap it around a telephone pole within three months. They knew these were sturdy, reliable cars, so that's what they chose."

Abigail felt a pang of guilt. She'd assumed he was born into wealth and privilege. "What happened to it?"

Storm grinned, looking a little sheepish. "I was going too fast on a gravel road. Totaled it within a month or two. I walked away without a scratch though. That is, until my dad got a hold of me." He laughed a deep, throaty laugh that sent pleasurable chills up Abigail's spine. She was beginning to see a glimpse of the man he really was when he was being himself and not trying to put on his Hollywood charm. She liked this version of him much better and felt smug satisfaction that she was likely one of the few to witness it.

Once Abigail pulled out of the parking garage and merged into the morning traffic, she realized she had no idea where they were going. "Your place or mine?" she asked, feeling a little wary. Had she even bothered to pick up after herself before she left that morning? Funny, L.A. traffic didn't faze her, but the thought of Storm seeing her house untidy was enough to cause her distress.

"I've got a better idea. I'll have my assistant book us in a suite at the Wylderton." When she started to protest, he said, "Relax. It's not what you think. I'm told their suites have two separate bedrooms and a spacious kitchenette. This will put us on neutral ground. You won't have to invite me to your place, and I'll spare you the details of my messy bachelor pad." It was a mild lie. His *bachelor pad* as he put it was far from messy, but he also knew his sprawling mansion might be intimidating and wanted to spare Abigail any unnecessary discomfort. He figured he'd already put her out enough.

"You're taking my boss's strange plan rather well." She stole a glance in his direction.

He was silent for a moment. "Honestly, I think I need this."

He looked doleful, and a little lost and Abigail resisted the urge to reach over and take his hand in hers. Instead she muttered under her breath, then darted around an aging sports car before cutting back into the far, right lane in front of a stretch limo. She offered no apologies for her aggressive driving. The mid-morning commuters could be downright hostile but she fit right in with them.

Storm smiled to himself. He liked driving fast and was impressed the old sedan could keep up with the flow of traffic. He dug into his pocket and pulled out his cell. "Call Patty," he spoke into the phone, then put his hand over the receiver and mouthed to Abigail, "My assistant."

"Patty, sweetheart, how are you? Listen kiddo, I need a huge favor, can you do that for me?" From somewhere inside, Abigail fumed in silence. Storm Jackson's Hollywood persona was back. He was lathering on the charm and crooning in a way that seemed to make all the ladies weak in the knees. It only angered Abigail; for reasons she couldn't fully explain. The persona seemed dishonest somehow. It seemed beneath him.

When he was off the phone, she returned the smile to her face. "Which way to the Wylderton?" she asked cheerily. Too cheerily. She would make a lousy actress.

CHAPTER TWO

Someone must have tipped off the press because by the time Abigail and Storm arrived outside the luxurious Wylderton hotel, the paparazzi were in full swing. Hotel security tried to shield the arriving guests from the chaos, but the upscale courtyard was a frenzied sea of cameras, reporters, and curious bystanders. Since Abigail had asked Storm to text her boss to let her know where they would be staying, and this was free publicity, she figured Tammie was the likely tipster and she glanced warily over at Storm to see if he looked annoyed.

His handsome face didn't hold a trace of anger or annoyance. Grinning instead, he reached over and patted her hand. "You ready for this?"

She nodded but found herself once again embarrassed by her faithful car—and worse, silently cursing herself for the casual jeans and worn-out sneakers she'd thrown on that morning. That morning she'd been trying to make a statement with her wardrobe choice. She sighed, realizing she was about to thoroughly succeed.

"You look amazing," Storm told her, as if sensing her apprehension. His comment was genuine, with no trace of his charming facade.

She made a face, then flashed him a grin. "I'm ready."

When they pulled up to the lavish front entrance, a valet rushed to her door, opening it for her. She handed over her keys with as much pride as she could muster as a Rolls-Royce pulled up behind her. "Don't go taking this for a joyride," she teased the valet.

"No ma'am," the young man responded dryly but a smiled tugged at the corners of his mouth.

Storm walked around to her side of the car and took her by the hand. Once he'd helped her to her feet, he leaned in and whispered something nonsensical into her ear. Abigail tried to ignore the quivering sensation that ran down to her toes. She moved closer to him and rubbed her cheek on his shoulder. "For the cameras," she whispered. Perhaps she could do this acting thing after all.

The lobby was an impressive spectacle of crystal chandeliers, polished marble tile, and magnificent oil paintings displayed in gold frames. Majestic palm trees thrust out from a glorious fountain in the center atrium. Uniformed staff bustled about checking in guests, arranging luggage, and manning the elevators. The guests had their own stately presence as they floated about in their designer shoes and beautifully tailored clothing. But it all paled in comparison to Storm, who strode confidently through the lobby doors with cameras flashing behind him and Abigail on his arm.

They didn't have to check in at the front desk—a first for Abigail but clearly the norm for Storm. A bellhop met them in the lobby. He offered to take their bags and looked slightly befuddled when they revealed they had none. The man slipped them their keycard and Storm gave him a generous tip, declining the bellhop's invitation to show them to their room.

When they stepped into the hotel suite, it was like stepping into a palace. Even the lobby hadn't prepared Abigail for all its splendor. It wasn't just amazing; it was *beyond* amazing. She had planned to appear unimpressed, but she couldn't help but gush as she walked from room to room, admiring the posh furnishings and high-end décor. The elegantly textured walls were painted in rich, warm tones. Tropical plants and luxurious urns adorned every corner.

"Storm, this is beautiful." She skimmed her fingertips across the enormous, fresh floral arrangement on the dining room table. She leaned into it, breathing in the aroma of hibiscus and orchids. A welcome basket sat beside it, filled to the brim with chocolates, fruit, and a bottle of champagne. "So, this is how the *other half* lives?" she quipped, then immediately regretted it, figuring he'd heard that line more times than he cared to count.

He didn't seem to mind though. "It's pretty great, right?" He was grinning widely, a bright, Hollywood-worthy grin, and appeared pleased she liked the accommodations.

"You stay here a lot?" she asked, not really wanting to know the answer. She tried to recall if she'd seen a tabloid with him entering or leaving the Wylderton.

"Nah. It's too pricey," he chuckled. Then his eyes narrowed and he inched towards her. "I've never met anyone quite worth the money until now." His demeanor had changed. He was suddenly all sex appeal and charisma. He placed a hand on Abigail's shoulder and gazed at her, his eyes smoldering into hers. He marveled that her eyes were both inquisitive and warm.

Here we go, Abigail thought, reminding herself to breathe as she felt her senses heighten at the softness of his touch. "Spare me," she managed, gently brushing his hand away. "How often does that line actually work, anyways?" She tried to appear unfazed and hoped the hammering of her heart wasn't audible.

Storm laughed and shrugged his shoulders, unoffended. "Every time until now, I guess." He rubbed his chin in thought. "Maybe I'm losing my touch."

"Oh, don't be too hard on yourself," she said, smiling. "I'm sure that'll still work on most."

He grinned back at her. "Should we, um, watch T.V. or something?"

"I'm actually starving," she admitted, remembering she'd skipped breakfast and it was now approaching lunchtime. She wondered if she could afford the room service in such a high-end place.

"I'll take you out to eat," he offered, looking delighted at the prospect.

"I'm not sure. There's all of those cameras, and then my car…" She trailed off, suddenly feeling inadequate. She hated the feeling. Confidence wasn't something she typically lacked.

"I have a car service and I know how to sneak past the cameras."

She raised an eyebrow. "Judging by the amount of times you've been in the tabloids, I'd say perhaps that skill needs a little honing."

"Hey," he said, grinning. "There's no such thing as bad publicity."

"Your agent and the studio would appear to disagree with you," she reminded him as she tried to keep the amusement out of her voice.

Storm chuckled, his deep, alluring laugh, and Abigail grinned back at him.

"Where did you have in mind?" she asked.

"There is this great, hole-in-the-wall Italian restaurant I know of—Cattaneo's. Quiet, candlelit dinner for two…" He paused when he realized Abigail looked hesitant once again. "Relax. I'm not trying to seduce you," he said, sounding a little offended. "I think you'd like the tranquility of the place is all."

"It's not that," she said, looking down at her tattered sneakers. "I just don't know if what I'm wearing…"

Storm stepped toward her. In the brief time he'd worked with her, he'd never known Abigail to get self-conscious about anything. Press conferences, work pressures, even his advances—she'd sailed through it all with poise. He found it fascinating and slightly alluring to discover she had a chink in her armor. Playfully, he stroked his chin as he looked her up and down. "Well," he decided, "I think you look beautiful, but I can have something sent up if you'd like."

"I couldn't let you do that." She lowered her eyes to glare at her sneakers.

He cupped her chin in his hand, lifting it until her eyes met his. "It would honestly be my pleasure."

She peered into his soft, blue-green eyes and tried not to melt. This was going to be a long couple of weeks. "Okay," she conceded. "I'll let you spoil me a little. I am, after all, giving up my life for two whole weeks." With some difficulty, she tore her eyes away from his gaze and pretended all at once to be interested in the hand-woven 18th Century tapestry hanging above the entryway table.

The concierge sent up a lavish collection of gowns from the hotel boutique for her to choose from. There was an assortment of short but elegant dresses in reds and blacks with sweetheart necklines or cutout backs. A wine-colored, mid-calf evening gown with a flared hemline. Longer, more formal gowns in various colors of chiffon or silk. Amongst the dresses were designer heels in Abigail's size, a bag of toiletries for the two of them, and a sizeable, obviously expensive, suitcase.

"What's in the fancy suitcase?" Abigail asked.

Storm shrugged. "Just some of my things."

She shot him a bewildered look. "How in the world did you manage that?"

"My assistant dropped it off. She knows what I like."

She shook her head, smiling. "You really do live a charmed life, don't you?"

Grinning back at her, he said, "It has its perks." He nodded his head towards the dresses slung over Abigail's arm. "Want me to help you pick one out?"

"I'm perfectly capable of picking one out on my own, thank you very much." Hearing the unintended harshness in her tone, she added,

"You'll just have to be surprised." She shot him a wink, picked up the designer shoes from the sofa, then scurried to her room before Storm could offer to help her undress and before, in a moment of famished weakness, she could say *yes*.

After careful consideration, Abigail chose a simple, black dress that stopped above her knees. It boasted a modest neckline, but the back swooped low, directly above her buttocks. The dress fit perfectly, as if it was tailored for her. With Storm's connections, perhaps it was.

When she walked out of her private master bedroom, Storm clutched a hand over his chest and pretended to stumble backwards, as if caught off-balance. Abigail figured he probably performed that little stunt a lot, but pretended it was just for her.

"You look gorgeous," he said. His eyes darkened with lust.

"Thank you." Careful to avoid being caught in his alluring gaze, she performed a slow twirl, showing off the lowcut back of the dress and the incredibly high heels.

"God almighty," he chuckled, and she couldn't stop herself from laughing at his dramatics. She noticed he had changed into a fresh shirt, but everything else was the same. She tried not to stare, realizing he'd look good wearing a paper sack. Or nothing. She dismissed her errant thoughts and reminded herself once again to keep things professional.

Storm took her by the hand as they stepped into the hallway. "Keep low and follow my lead."

The pair raced down the hallway, crouching and peering around every turn—more for dramatic flair than out of necessity. Giggling like school children and out of breath, they rode the service elevator to the parking garage. When they stepped out of the elevator and opened the heavy doors to the parking garage, a sleek, black sedan waited for them by the curb. There wasn't a driver in sight, and Abigail shot Storm a weary look.

"Get in," he told her, opening the passenger door for her.

"Okay, but let's hope you're a better driver than you were in your youth."

"Oh Cricket, I'm much, much worse." He laughed wickedly, screeching away from the curb and speeding in the direction of the brightly illuminated exit sign.

CHAPTER THREE

Cattaneo's Ristorante did not disappoint. The mouthwatering smell of fresh baked bread, buttery sauces, and hints of oregano and basil wafted down the street, beckoning people through the wooden bistro doors to taste the authentic Italian cuisine. The harmonic sound of the mandolin and accordion magnified the allure.

The hostess showed the pair to a small table in the back. Nobody in the restaurant seemed to recognize Storm, or they were too polite to let on if they did. The perfect gentleman, he pulled back Abigail's chair, pushed it back in as she took a seat, then sat down across from her. He smoothed his hands through his dark, wavy hair as he grinned back at her.

"What?" she asked, trying to ascertain the reason behind the smirk on his gorgeous face.

"When you woke up this morning, is this how you imagined spending your day?"

She laughed and scrunched her forehead, thinking about her morning and how she'd wanted to crawl back into bed to avoid whatever discussion her boss had wanted to have about Storm—her *assignment.* She gazed back at him, considering how quickly she was shifting from thinking of him as just an assignment. Then she shook the thought away and lifted the menu.

"So, what's good here?" she asked, not answering his question.

"Everything." He flashed a wicked grin and plucked the menu from her hand. "But I had them whip us up something special."

Ordinarily, Abigail would be annoyed with someone ordering for her, but Storm looked so excited and she was impressed he'd taken the time to prearrange something. *He probably does this all the time*, the cynical part of her brain told her, but she pushed the thought away.

"What are we having tonight?"

"I had them make sample portions of all my favorite dishes. Trust me, you will love everything."

When the first course was brought out, she was a little skeptical. "Ravioli?"

"Trust me, this isn't like any ravioli you've ever had," he said, lifting his fork to his lips and shoveling a large helping into his mouth.

She shrugged, placed a small portion on her fork, and took a timid bite. The flavors exploded in her mouth—a delectable assault on her taste buds. She practically hummed aloud with appreciation. "Oh, my gosh."

"I told you." Storm beamed at her, taking pleasure in the innocent way her eyes closed when she paused to enjoy her first bite.

When the second course arrived, a traditional manicotti drizzled with olive oil and dusted with freshly grated Parmesan, Abigail dug in hungrily. "This is amazing," she spoke with a mouthful of food.

"Sorry," she said once she'd swallowed the bite whole and dabbed her lips with her cloth napkin. "Me and my table manners."

He grinned at her with admiration. "Hey, I don't think there's anything sexier than a woman with a healthy appetite."

"Really? *That's* what you find most sexy?" she asked doubtfully as her thoughts flickered to all the reed-thin, long-legged beauties she'd seen him with in the papers who looked like they'd skipped a meal or two as a matter of routine.

He nodded. "Absolutely." When she still looked doubtful, he asked, "What do you find sexy?"

"Honestly?" She took a generous drink of Cabernet Sauvignon, enjoying its blackberry overtones, while she paused to consider.

"Yeah," he challenged, returning his fork to his plate and gazing back at her as he waited patiently for her reply.

"A man with a book in his hand," she said decidedly.

"Seriously?" It was his turn to look skeptical.

"Yes." She tossed her hair over her shoulder, eyes gleaming. "I remember about a month back I was waiting in a drive-thru at a coffee shop. This guy walked out to the patio, clutching a book, and he took a seat at a table all by himself. He wore these absurdly large glasses and had that sort of Jerry curl on his forehead. You know, someone who would probably be considered a nerd by most people's standards. But I found myself staring as he opened his book and just got lost in the pages. And I thought to myself, now there's a man comfortable enough in his own skin to sit all by himself and just do what makes him happy."

She paused to take a sip of water. "Plus, let's face it," she said with a shrug, "with some of the men I've dated over the years, it's nice to know right from the beginning if the man actually knows how to read."

Storm chuckled, then fell silent, pondering. "You know what I think?" he said dryly.

"What?"

He leaned in closer, as if he was about to say something so profound, only she should hear it. "I think if you had time to sit in your car and take all that in while waiting to order a cup of coffee, you need to visit a more efficient coffee shop."

Abigail burst out laughing at his unexpected comment. "Well, you're a hopeless romantic." For a moment she let her gaze settle on the adorable laugh lines surrounding his gorgeous, turquoise eyes. Then, with some difficulty, she redirected her attention to the new course being set in front of her.

"Would you mind taking a picture of us?" Storm asked a waiter passing by, handing over his phone before scooting his chair closer to Abigail's.

She shot him a questioning look but leaned in closer to him. He slipped an arm around her shoulders and they both smiled as the phone camera flashed. Patrons from nearby tables smiled and leaned in closer to take their own photos—revealing they recognized Storm after all.

"Thanks," he said politely, retrieving the phone from the waiter and handing him a tip in its stead. He scrolled through the pictures, smiled, then handed his phone over to Abigail. "Which one do you like?"

Still confused, she took the phone and scrolled through the photos. The incandescent lighting of the restaurant cast a warm, soft glow. It made the setting look all the more intimate. She loved the pictures if she was being honest. Between Storm's million-dollar smile and the way his arm was slung casually over her shoulders, she could almost pretend they were on a real date.

"What did you want a picture for?" she asked, trying to sound nonchalant as she scrolled back through for a second look.

"I need to send one to my assistant. After Harry fired my publicist, Patty helps manage my social media accounts."

"Oh," she said flatly, handing the phone back. "I like the third one."

"Oh, I'm sorry, I should have asked first. Are you comfortable with that? I just figured if we wanted our relationship to look real…"

She silently scolded herself for being disappointed. This was a job. For both of them. She needed to remember that. "Oh, no, of course it's fine. I had forgotten my firm agreed to allow you to maintain control of your social media accounts. Usually, for my clients, I get a junior staffer to take that over so we can avoid any … surprises." She smiled sweetly back at him and tried to suppress the hurt she knew she had no business feeling. She'd walked into that restaurant knowing their intimate dining experience was all a ruse. She just hadn't expected to become so *painfully* aware.

The remaining courses were equally satisfying—and each was paired with a different wine to complement the food. Italian Chianti, with its bold flavors to enhance the marinara sauce of the chicken parmesan. A hearty Sangiovese to accompany the creaminess of the pasta carbonara. The earthiness of the Pinot Noir was a perfect match to the chef's prize-winning mushroom risotto. Although she tried to pace herself, by the final course, Abigail was feeling a little tipsy and uncomfortably full. "I need to stop," she said breathlessly.

Laughing, Storm reached across the table and squeezed her hand. Sobered, she instinctively pulled it away.

"Ouch." He frowned in her direction, looking puzzled.

"I'm sorry." She let herself relax again. "I just want to make sure we keep this professional."

"You got it, Cricket." His response was smooth, as if he wasn't at all bothered by her statement—something that both irritated and confounded her.

She was quiet on the stroll back to the car, uncertain how one ended the perfect, make-believe date.

"I had a great time today," Storm told her as he opened the car door for her.

"Me too," she admitted aloud once they were both inside the car. Again, she couldn't help but wonder how many other women he'd taken to that same restaurant.

"I've never taken anyone there before," he said, as if reading her private thoughts. "It's just such an intimate setting, I didn't want anyone to discover it. When I'm there I can relax and let my guard down." He lapsed into silence and Abigail reached across the seat and slipped her hand in his.

"I really did have a nice time," she told him. She gave his hand a gentle squeeze, then quickly returned her hand to her lap.

Storm smiled and the tension in the car dissipated. As he pulled the car away from the curb, he shifted the topic to how he got into acting and Abigail listened intently despite her foggy head. Each time Storm laughed aloud at a past memory, or stole a glance in her direction, she felt him take a piece of her heart. And in her semi-inebriated state, she wasn't in any position to hold onto the pieces.

When they reached the hotel, she was feeling sleepy from her overindulgence of food and wine. Before the valet could open her door, Storm was out of the car and opening it for her. He leaned in, took her hand, and pressed it to his lips before helping her out of the car.

Abigail turned to face him. She shivered with pleasure at the way his eyes burned into hers. "I'm starting to see the appeal," she confessed, flushing only a little. She could blame it on the haze of the alcohol, but she knew it wouldn't be the truth.

Storm traced her lips with his thumb, then bent down and pressed his lips to hers. Before she could lean into the kiss, he playfully swept her into his arms and spun her around before releasing her again to stand on her own two, unsteady feet. "For the cameras," he explained, although there weren't any around.

CHAPTER FOUR

*F*eeling slightly hung over, Abigail padded out of her room and into the living space she temporarily shared with Storm. He was lounging on the couch, shirtless and wearing threadbare sweatpants and somehow managing to look amazing. A silver tray rested in the middle of the coffee table and she noted with appreciation that he'd ordered them coffee.

She sat in a chair across from him, wearing the jeans, t-shirt, and sneakers from the morning before. "I hope this coffee didn't set you back too much," she said.

"What do you mean?"

"I mean if you can no longer afford a shirt." She raised an eyebrow in amusement and he grinned wickedly back at her.

Reaching for the creamer, her hand froze and her smile faded when she spotted the newspaper skillfully placed to the right of the coffee tray.

"Oh, my word," was all she managed. She plucked the paper from its resting place and read the headline.

'*Storm Jackson: Who Is She to Him?*' And there was Abigail, all smiles as she held Storm's hand in front of the Wylderton. Thanks to the blurred, semi-pixilated photograph, she knew it would be hard for others to recognize her. But she recognized herself all too well. Tall, slender, and blonde—she recognized the cliché she was. Disappointed in herself, she bit down hard on her bottom lip as she fought back frustrated tears.

"I think you look good," Storm mumbled, looking down at his coffee cup. Abigail thought he seemed offended, somehow.

"Sorry, I'm just not used to seeing myself in the papers," she lied. That wasn't the issue at all. She'd probably need to call her mother and explain. If anyone could recognize her, her mother could. Then again, the binding nondisclosure agreement she'd signed when she'd taken him on as a client prohibited her from explaining.

"Relax," Storm joked. "When this is all over, you can tell the world you dumped me."

His comment inspired a laugh from her. "Yeah, I'm sure everyone would believe that." She fell silent for a moment. She wanted to explain that her reaction to the article had nothing to do with him and everything to do with her. Instead, she said, "We should probably swing by my place today. I need to pick up some clothes."

He shot her a mischievous grin. "I think you should keep wearing that dress from last night."

Color rushed to her cheeks. "You'll probably find my actual wardrobe just a tad disappointing," she said with a laugh.

Storm took inventory of how she filled out her faded blue jeans and the enticing way her thin t-shirt rested against her breasts. He decided he doubted that statement very much.

Located in a quiet suburb outside of Los Angeles, Abigail had loved her cottage-style home from the moment she'd laid eyes on it. She was pleased with the landscaping she'd done herself (well, with a little help from her mother) and prided herself on having a tasteful eye when it came to decorating. Yet somehow, the thought of Storm seeing the house gave her the same feeling of inadequacy she'd had when she'd realized he'd be riding in her car. When they pulled into the gravel driveway, she put her car into park and stole a glance at him.

"We're here," she announced unnecessarily.

Storm got out of the car, breathing in the welcoming scent of orange blossom and stretching his long legs before looking around. He soaked in the exterior charm of Abigail's 1 ½ story home with its quaint, wrap-around porch and prominent chimney. He admired the shingled roof and the exterior's traditional mix of grayish-taupe siding and stone. The front door had been painted an inviting navy blue. It balanced the exterior's otherwise neutral color pallet. "Now *this* place feels like a home."

His enthusiasm made Abigail smile. That's exactly what she'd thought when the realtor first showed her the place. With renewed confidence, she led him onto the porch and through the front entryway.

"I apologize upfront if it's a mess. I had to leave in a hurry yesterday because my boss insisted that she needed to meet with me about an *important* client." She was all cheerful sarcasm as she winked in his direction.

"I'm kind of a pain, aren't I?" he asked genuinely, but began to show himself around without waiting for a reply.

"Do you offer your services as a decorator too?" he shouted from somewhere down the hallway. "Seriously, I could use someone."

"I'd be happy to take a look," Abigail yelled over her shoulder from her bedroom where she was busily stuffing clothes into a suitcase. Jeans, t-shirts, sundresses, evening attire. She threw in several pairs of bras and panties, smiling to herself as she added a newly purchased black, lacy bra and matching thong panties to the mix.

"The house really looks great." She jumped. Storm was directly behind her, murmuring the words into her ear. She calmed herself and turned to face him.

"Decorating is sort of a hobby of mine. I'd love to help. Free of charge," she told him, winking again. She was starting to think she was developing a nervous tic around him. He probably thought she had something in her eye. A blush crept into her cheeks and she looked away.

"You're sort of adorable," he said matter of fact, then wandered off to look at the rest of the house, leaving Abigail breathless.

"I'm ready," she finally announced, plunking down her overpacked suitcase in the living room. "Dang, that is heavy."

He came up behind her again and began to rub the tension from her shoulders. When he bent down and kissed the back of her right shoulder, Abigail tensed. "Relax, Cricket" he teased. "I'll be a gentleman." Without another word, he picked up her bag and headed toward the front door.

"What's the game plan for tonight?" she asked as they drove back to the hotel.

"I have that benefit banquet for the new wing of the children's hospital."

"Ooh, maybe the press can get a shot of you writing a big fat check. Or better yet, maybe they'll name the new wing after you. That would help your image." She was teasing him, of course. Her heart melted a little at the thought of Storm giving up his evening to help children. But then a different, more selfish thought popped into her head and she blurted out, "Crap, now I need to find something else to wear." She turned to him and pretended to pout. "And you let the boutique take back all those pretty dresses."

Storm smiled slyly to himself.

"What did you do?" She looked over at him, flashing a circumspect smile.

"You'll see."

To her relief, there weren't any paparazzi at the hotel entrance. To be safe, the pair took the service elevator once more and slipped quietly into their hotel suite. Laying over the couch in the front room were two gorgeous gowns—one black, one green. Next to them was a pair of black, strappy stiletto heels that would flatter either dress.

"Storm, you didn't have to do this," Abigail said, admiring the gowns that probably cost more than her monthly salary.

"This is too much," she continued, but she was already slipping off her socks and sneakers to try on the shoes.

"I think the green dress will match perfectly with your eyes," he said, and she rolled her eyes in response.

"Hey, it's not a line," he laughed, holding up his hands in surrender. "You choose."

She did choose the green one. It was snug in all the right places and accentuated her curves. While the back was not quite as revealing as the dress she previously wore, the neckline plunged well below where she was typically comfortable—but somehow it still looked elegant as opposed to inappropriate. She curled her hair. A rarity for her, but she liked the way the curls softened her features. When Storm knocked on her door, she invited him in. *Be strong. Be strong.* She mouthed the words silently to herself.

He entered the room, carrying a necklace with a delicate, pear-shaped emerald. "May I?" he asked, but he was already moving her honey-blonde curls aside and slipping the necklace around her swanlike neck.

"It's perfect," she murmured, fingering the smooth stone.

"I couldn't agree more." He kissed the back of her shoulder once again. This time Abigail turned around to face him, tipping her head back so her eyes met his. Storm skimmed his knuckles down her cheek, then bent down and kissed her in the same spot his knuckles had grazed. Her skin warmed at his touch and she felt the blood rush to her ears. She knew she should stop him, but she didn't think she had the strength. Instead, her hand reached to his hair and she trailed her fingers through it. She gazed up at him with those *come and kiss me* eyes, and he found himself compelled to oblige.

Growling with desire, Storm crushed his lips down on hers. Abigail gasped with anticipation. She threw her arms around his neck as she stood on her tiptoes to meet his kiss. She closed her eyes and could feel herself getting lost in his advances. Then a sudden image of the tabloids popped into her head and she took a step backwards, gently pushing him away.

"I'm sorry, I can't."

He looked disappointed, hurt even, but he cleared his throat and said, "Hey, no pressure. I get it." He turned to walk out of the room. "Dress looks great on you, Cricket," he said casually over his shoulder.

It took Abigail a few minutes to compose herself before she left her room. When she did, she found Storm lounging lazily on the couch, his feet propped on a pillow. He had changed into a tux, minus the jacket, and appeared preoccupied with a private texting conversation. A mischievous smile played across his face as he responded in text-speak to whomever the lucky recipient was.

Abigail fumed from within. Clearly Storm had a short attention span. "I'm ready," she announced, probably too bluntly.

He glanced up at her, looking bored. He sat up on the couch, tossed his cellphone on the table, then picked up a piece of paper. "I had the front desk print you a copy of the itinerary my assistant prepared. Here are the parties, interviews, and other obligations I'll be attending over the next two weeks. Please, look them over, and let me know if you have any conflicts. There are a few things we can probably reschedule if needed." His tone was all business and she felt oddly disappointed. Wasn't this what she'd wanted?

She took the piece of paper, resisting the urge to snatch it from his hand. After studying it, she said, "Looks fine. I'll let you know if a conflict comes up." Her words were void of emotion.

"You ready to go then, Cricket?" He rose from the couch and slipped into the tuxedo jacket carefully laid over a chair.

Abigail tried to pretend she didn't notice the way his muscles filled out the wool designer jacket. Or how the silk pocket square perfectly matched his eyes. He looked stunning, yet he spoke to her with such indifference, it left a dull ache inside her. *Silly girl, pull yourself together*, she silently scolded herself. "Ready as I'll ever be," she said aloud, forcing a smile.

CHAPTER FIVE

*A*bigail was silent on the limo ride to the benefit, but Storm appeared oblivious. He asked the driver to turn up the music and even sang along on occasion. His voice was low, and smooth as honey. To Abigail, it was comforting, confusing, and maddening all at once.

"Is this too loud?" he asked above the music, but she shook her head *no* and stared out the window. When her favorite song came on, she resisted the urge to sing along. Just as she resisted the urge to lean over and kiss him, or to grab his hand and pull it close to hers. She fought off the desire to climb into his lap and let him have his way with her—screw the *just business* routine. Wasn't she allowed to have fun? But she suppressed all these feelings as she sat in silence and stared out at the passing cars, permitting only one small tear to escape and seep down her cheek before she quickly brushed it away.

The sheer volume of paparazzi waiting for them when they arrived at the benefit took Abigail by surprise and her heart leapt into her throat. Cameras flashed and reporters clamored for the perfect shot from behind the velvet ropes. The red carpet was rolled out, exactly the way she'd seen on T.V. many times before.

"You get used to it," Storm said, sensing her apprehension. He gave her hand a reassuring squeeze. The back door of the limo opened, and a crowd of people screamed once they realized it was Storm Jackson in the backseat. Appearing unfazed, he exited the car, then turned and took Abigail by the hand once more. "We'll get through this together," he said, winking at her as he helped her out of the car.

He held her hand firmly in his as he strode easily down the red carpet, smiling at the cameras and waving with his free hand. Abigail watched him magically make the switch to acting mode—boyish charm and Hollywood smile. She attempted to do the same, offering short, timid waves as she plastered on a smile.

Abigail endeavored to look graceful as Storm led her down the long, carpeted walkway and through the massive doors of the old mansion turned museum that housed the benefit.

"You did great," he told her when they were out of view from most of the camera crews. She studied him to see if he was being patronizing, but he was all smiles. "Really, you were a natural, Cricket." She was beginning to hate the nickname. It reminded her of how insignificant she really was to him. A small, insignificant bug. Gross.

"Thank you," she said, forcing a smile she hoped looked genuine.

At the banquet Storm moved easily through the crowd, introducing Abigail as his *date* or *companion* but avoiding the word girlfriend. Clearly, he was even afraid of pretend commitment, she thought bitterly, but she turned on her own charm and worked the crowd. Amongst the distinguished guests were famous politicians, actors and athletes alike—as well as California's most influential business leaders.

Abigail appeared to listen intently to the buzzing conversations, laughing when appropriate, and adding a few stories of her own. Her stories were perhaps a bit embellished, but then she suspected so were those of the other guests. All the while she surveyed the room's fancy linens, high-priced champagne, and expensive hors d'oeuvres. As she looked around at the designer gowns, likely purchased special for the evening, she wondered how much more could have been raised for charity if the guests opened their checkbooks without having to be wined and dined in such high-class fashion.

She shouldn't judge, she knew that. She imagined most people in the room worked hard for their money and perhaps needed a little coaxing to be parted with such large sums of it. She also realized the media coverage of their attendance at the event would boost charitable contributions beyond that evening's benefit. Still, the entire scene seemed a bit shallow and she wondered how Storm could stand it. She found it exhausting.

After an hour of endless conversation, she politely excused herself to grab another drink from the bar. She was already buzzing but decided to break her two-drink rule for the second time that week. When she turned away from the bar to face the crowd again, she spotted Storm from across the room, chatting intimately with a dark-

haired beauty with ruby red lips and a snug-fitting dress that left little
to the imagination.

Her first instinct was to rush to his side and whisk him away, but
she hung back, waiting to see what he would do. Even with the
distance between them, she could tell Storm was laying the charm on
thick. He touched the girl's bare shoulder and laughed at something
she said. Abigail crossed the floor in the direction of the hors
d'oeuvres table, snatching up an unrecognizable morsel of food and
popping it into her mouth. Her eyes watered. It tasted awful, but she
managed to swallow it, then drained the rest of her glass to wash the
unwelcome taste from her mouth.

A waiter walked by with a tray of fruity drinks and she grabbed
one, guzzling down half of the glass before coming up for air. *Pace
yourself*, she muttered under her breath. But it was too late. The assault
of the alcohol was already giving her the spins. Her eyes darted around
the museum for the ladies' room. When she spotted the sign, she made
her way to it, slipping through the crowd.

Within the restroom, she grabbed a handful of paper towels, ran
cold water over them, then dabbed her cheeks and forehead. She was
thankful she'd opted for minimal makeup because she was quite
certain she'd look affright otherwise. She could imagine her picture in
all the magazines, the makeup dripping down her jealous face.

Who is she? She remembered the latest headline. *I'm no one*, she
thought, as if she needed the reminder.

Leaving the restroom, she scanned the crowd but didn't see any
sign of Storm. Her heart sank to her toes when she noticed the
staircase and the dark hallways of the second floor. A velvet rope

marked the stairway as closed, but there was plenty of room to get around it. She imagined Storm, hidden in the corner of one of the second-floor rooms, his hands on the brunette woman as he kissed her and whispered his charming flatteries.

Remembering it was her job to protect Storm from his womanizing ways, Abigail squared her shoulders and squeezed around the rope barricade. As she headed up the steps, a security guard tried to stop her, but before she could protest, Storm appeared at the top of the staircase. "She's with me," he said smoothly, and the guard stepped aside and let her pass.

She was relieved to find he was alone. "Where's your lady friend?" she asked friendly enough. But the biting sarcasm was there, just beneath the surface.

"Who?" he asked innocently. A smile played at the corners of his mouth, but quickly disappeared.

Abigail put her hands on her hips and tilted her head to the side, but she couldn't help but smile. Flirting came naturally to Storm. And being irresistibly charming came just as easily she supposed. "I can't take you anywhere, can I?" she teased.

"You're right Cri-." He paused. "You're right, Abigail," he amended. He liked that she didn't appear to judge. She knew better than anyone about his vices, yet she didn't fault him.

Storm closed the gap between them. He trailed his hand down her arm until his fingertips brushed hers. Then he took her slender hand in his. "Come on, I want to show you something." He slipped into a nearby room, closed the door, then flicked on the lights.

Abigail blinked twice, her eyes adjusting to the light, then she looked around. They were in a beautiful, old library room. The walls were lined with heavy wooden shelving that held hundreds of antique, leather-bound books. She closed her eyes again and inhaled deeply. "I love the smell of old books."

"I do too," he said, taking her by surprise.

"Are you a reader?" she quizzed him.

"Well, I *can* read." His turquoise eyes danced with humor.

"You know what I mean."

"I don't get to read as often as I'd like, but it is one of my favorite things to do when it's quiet."

"I would never have pegged you as a reader," she admitted, thinking back to when she'd told him she found reading sexy. "It seems too... too..."

"Too...?" Storm asked, raising an eyebrow and grinning.

"Low-key."

"I guess you don't know me like you think you do." There was the faintest hint of bitterness in his tone and Abigail found herself reaching for his hand and pulling him closer to her.

"I'm sorry," she said. "I'm just... careful."

"So I've gathered." The bitterness was gone, replaced by a boyish grin. It was his genuine smile; the one Abigail was convinced was reserved for her. Not the overly charming one he flashed to the crowds and cameras.

Storm couldn't help but gawk as he studied her. Wideset, green eyes that shone with passion and intrigue. Slightly pointed chin that complemented her high cheekbones. Generous mouth that revealed two faint dimples whenever she smiled. Hard as he tried, he could no longer feign his indifference. "I find you fascinating, Miss Travis."

"And I find you…"

"What? Charming? Clever?" His eyes bore into hers. "Irresistible?" He plucked a book from the shelf and clutched it to his chest. "Sexy?" he teased.

"Annoying," she said flatly, but her face lit up into a smile.

Storm set the book back on the shelf, then moved in closer, tempting her with his gaze.

Abigail took a step back. "Look, I like you," she found herself admitting aloud. "Which is what makes this so difficult for me. I have to keep this professional. When these two weeks are over, we'll go our separate ways. Whatever these feelings that are creeping up, they're not real. It's just what happens when two people spend a great deal of time together and know any intimacy is forbidden. It's human nature to want what you can't have. You'll see." She didn't actually believe any of the words she spoke, but she said them with enough conviction she felt certain Storm was convinced she believed them.

"I guess you have us all figured out then," he said softly. He didn't sound bitter. He sounded regretful. Misunderstood.

She wanted to take back her words, but instead she smiled and took his hand. "Come on," she said with as much enthusiasm as she could muster. "Let's rejoin the party. If I'm not mistaken, you've got a big fat check to write."

"Lead the way, darlin'." His demeanor was back to his Hollywood-style charm and Abigail felt herself grow cold inside.

CHAPTER SIX

"That was exhausting," Storm admitted once they were safely back inside the limo. He loosened his bow tie and let it hang loosely from his neck, sighing with relief as the limo driver pulled away from the curb.

Abigail gave him an inquisitive look. "Really? You looked like you were having a great time."

"Oh, yes, the life of a big-time movie star. All parties and limelight. Spending all my time being someone I'm not." Storm leaned back in his seat and looked over at her. "You know, you think you get to quit acting when the director yells, *cut*, but it never ends. Sometimes it feels like my whole life is one big act." For the first time Abigail noticed his words were a little slurred.

"You're drunk," she observed, trying not to sound like she was judging.

"You intoxicate me," he told her, leaning in closer. But it wasn't the real him, and she pushed him away.

"Save your lines for someone who actually buys them. You're not that great of an actor."

Her words were harsh and seemed to strike a nerve with Storm, who grew quiet.

She looked out the window and pretended not to notice, but guilt stirred inside her. She stole a glance and noticed him watching her.

"I didn't mean that," she finally said.

"No, you're right," he said with a shrug. "I suck at acting."

"No, you're a good actor."

"How do you know, you've never seen any of my movies, remember?" He looked at her, challenging her to refute her earlier statement.

"Yes, I have," she admitted quietly.

"What's that?" A wicked smile tugged at the corners of his kissable mouth.

"Yes I have," she said louder, thankful for the privacy screen between them and the front seat so nobody else could witness her mortification.

"But you said…" He feigned confusion.

"I lied." She practically shouted her admission. "I've seen almost all of your films. I think you're a brilliant actor, despite some of the corny, predictable plotlines. I think you're talented and amazing and have so much more to offer than you let on. I think that when you drop the Hollywood act, underneath is a kind, gentle man who has his own charisma no agent or acting coach can teach."

Abigail knew she should stop her ramblings there, but fueled by the feelings she'd kept bottled up since they'd first met, feelings that she'd almost convinced herself didn't exist but in actuality had been growing day by day, she continued her monologue of confession. "I hate that you feel like you always have to act like someone you're not. I hate that you don't get to be the carefree, amazing person that I know you could be. And I hate that if I act on my feelings for you, I'll be just another cliché. Another notch on your belt." By this point the tears were streaming down her face. Storm leaned over to pull her closer to him, but she scooted further away.

"Just don't," she said. "I'm a big girl. You don't need to comfort me."

The car came to a stop outside of the hotel. Abigail wiped her eyes, squared her shoulders, and scrambled out of the limo, not bothering to wait for the valet or for Storm. They took the elevator to their room in silence. Storm kept glancing at her as if he wanted to say something, but he remained quiet.

When they were standing in the hallway outside their suite, she reached for the door handle and Storm's hand closed over hers. "You could never be a cliché, Abigail."

She glanced up at him. Her eyes still glistened with tears, but her poised demeanor had returned. "It's okay, really. Just forget about it." Her voice was weak, but kind. She offered a wan smile, then stepped through the door and headed for her room. She stopped before she reached the door, then turned to face him. "I had a wonderful time being with you," she said. "I really mean that." Then she closed the door to her room, shutting him out and leaving him both confused and wanting.

CHAPTER SEVEN

$\mathcal{A}$wake and showered, Abigail wandered into the living room, fully expecting to find Storm in his sweatpants, sipping coffee. Instead she was disappointed to discover she was alone. The morning paper was sitting on the table, and she gingerly crossed the room to read it.

'Has Hollywood's Bad Boy Been Tamed?' the boldly printed headline read. And there she was, on the red carpet with Storm, their hands intertwined, both smiling and looking very much like a couple. At that moment, the door to their suite opened and Storm sauntered in, looking smug.

"Great headline, right?" he beamed.

"Yeah, just the kind of publicity you've been wanting." She smiled back, happy for him, but deep down she was disappointed in herself. To the outside world she looked like some sort of starstruck floozy. *You are acting like a starstruck floozy*, she reminded herself.

"I am sorry that I'm such a pain," he told her, seeing the hurt in her eyes she couldn't mask behind her pretty smile. "I've always known what's expected of me and sometimes it's just easier to live up to those expectations."

"Let's just get through this next two weeks, okay?" She smiled warmly but her words left a chill in the air. "I need to check in at work," she said, changing the subject and retreating to her room.

"Great job so far," Tammie chirped from the other end of the line. "People really think you're taming him."

"He's tamer than people think," Abigail said, defending him.

"Oh, please tell me you're not already sleeping with him. Puh-lease tell me that I wasn't wrong in thinking you could resist this...this... *actor.*"

"I'm not sleeping with him!" Abigail said, a little too loudly. She poked her head around the corner to be sure Storm hadn't heard her outburst. He appeared lost in a text messaging conversation. "I'm not sleeping with him," she said more quietly, and with more conviction. "I'm simply saying he's not as much of a bad-boy as the tabloids make him out to be."

Tammie was silent, as if rethinking her decision.

"I can handle this," Abigail reassured her, breaking the silence.

"Okay, well so far things are looking up, so I'll keep you on this. But I swear to you Abby, if you think you're getting in over your head, I can pull you from this assignment. I mean that. No questions asked. No reflection on your performance." Tammie had never referred to her as Abby before. She sounded genuinely concerned. For once Abigail got the impression her boss might actually be human.

"And for the sake of the company's reputation, please get some highlights in that hair." That was more like it, Abigail thought, chuckling as she hung up the phone.

"What's on the docket for today?" she asked casually when she rejoined Storm in the living room. She already knew what was on the schedule. Today Storm was doing an interview with Leslie Stokes to promote his upcoming film. Abigail was excited to see Leslie's show up close and personal, and even more excited to watch Storm in action, but she didn't let on.

Before he could answer, Abigail's cellphone rang and she ran back to her room to grab it.

"Have you lost your mind, Abby?" her mother started in the moment she answered the phone.

"Hello to you too, Mom," she laughed.

"This is serious honey. Now don't get me wrong, this guy is a major hunk, but sweetie, you're too good to allow any man to just use you and toss you aside."

"Mom, relax," she interrupted. "It's not what you think." She desperately wanted to tell her mother exactly what was going on so she wouldn't worry—but she was bound by a nondisclosure agreement.

"So, are you not dating him then?"

"Well, it's complicated, Mom. But can you just trust me when I say I know what I'm doing?"

Her mother hesitated. "Well, you've always had a good head on your shoulders. But darling, after the last two boys you dated, I thought by now you'd learn to pick a keeper."

Abigail rolled her eyes at her mother's choice of words. No matter how old she got, her mother always referred to any man she dated as a *boy*. Perhaps it made her feel younger.

It still pained Abigail a little to reflect on her last two failed relationships. Shawn Broun. He had been her first—a late-night tryst her sophomore year in college that had blossomed into a friendship and eventually a relationship that lasted the remainder of their college years. When she'd announced her plans to move back home to L.A. after graduation, Shawn offered to follow, despite her protests. She didn't want to be responsible for anyone uprooting their life.

Within six months after the move, it was evident Shawn wasn't cut out for California. Their relationship limped along for another few months, mostly out of convenience, but eventually the two parted ways—promising to remain friends and stay in touch, although they both knew that wouldn't happen. Other than the exchange of a few awkward emails, and a single box of forgotten items Abigail shipped to his new address, all contact ceased after the breakup.

About a year after moving back to L.A., Abigail met Anthony Thompson at a restaurant across the street from her office building. Anthony was charming and gorgeous and had a head full of dreams that, at first, she'd found endearing and inspirational. The couple began a whirlwind romance and within a few short months, Anthony moved into her too-small-for-two apartment.

Things were great at first. During the initial honeymoon phase of the relationship the apartment felt cozy and Anthony seemed ambitious. But in the months that followed it became clear to her he was far more of a dreamer than a visionary—making plans without much forethought and with far too much optimism. When he quit his job to *pursue* such dreams, Abigail held her tongue for as long as she could. But when the finances all fell to her, she began to resent him and had the distinct feeling she was suffocating each night she returned to their cramped apartment and found him lounging on the couch; the *Help Wanted* ads she'd strategically placed next to the sofa left unopened and unread.

After her breakup with Anthony, she'd vowed she wasn't going to waste any time with someone she didn't see herself having a future with. That was about a year ago. Since then she'd purchased her own home, and other than a blind date or two orchestrated by well-meaning friends and family members, she'd remained single.

"If my friend Eloise has seen this, she's going to think you've gone and lost all of your senses. You know she always believed you had such a good head on your shoulders." Her mother continued to dredge on.

"Mom just remember that you can't believe everything you read in the papers. Can you remember that for me?"

"Trouble at home?" Storm asked when Abigail reentered the room.

Her heart skipped a beat. "Did you hear all that?"

"Only a little bit. I wasn't eavesdropping I swear." But he gave her a sly, lopsided grin.

"My mother. She worries," Abigail explained. "She'll get over it."

"You could have told her the truth, you know. I don't mind."

"That's okay. I signed an NDA and I'm not one to go back on my word. Besides, this will all be over soon, and will be just a distant memory."

Storm was silent for a moment.

"I'm sorry, Storm, I didn't mean to imply that you were putting me out. I just meant…"

"It's Jack," he interrupted, his voice barely above a whisper.

"Huh?"

He cleared his throat, feeling nervous for reasons that escaped him. "My real name. It's not Storm. It's Jack."

Abigail stared at him for a moment to be certain he was being serious. Then, she burst out laughing. "Wait a minute. Your name is Jack Jackson?"

He couldn't help but laugh. "No, it's Jack Reid, actually. I thought you knew everything about me. It's in my bio." The corner of his eyes crinkled in amusement.

She threw up her hands in mock exasperation. "Oh, I'm sorry. I've been so busy trying to keep you out of trouble I haven't had time to do any leisure activities like, you know, reading."

He chuckled.

"Jack suits you," she said, changing the subject.

"No one refers to me by that name anymore, except for my sister, Lylah."

"What about your parents?"

"You really didn't read my bio at all, did you?"

Abigail flushed a little. "I was never very good at homework, I guess. Besides, the bio your agent sent over was quite lengthy. I had my assistant read it and provide a summary. Apparently, she left a little out."

He chuckled once again. "That's alright. I'm not offended. It's sort of refreshing, actually. Most of the time it seems like the women I meet know more about me, or *think* they know more about me, than I do." He was smiling but Abigail suspected it bothered him more than he let on.

"So, what's the story with your parents?" she asked, hoping she wasn't being too indelicate.

"Oh, they're still around. They just never agreed with the whole acting thing. My father thinks it's an immoral and lazy way to make a living. And my mother … well … my mother thinks whatever my father thinks." The smile remained on his handsome face, but Abigail could see the sadness in his eyes as he spoke.

He continued. "I left home as soon as I was of age and never looked back. Sure, I talk to my parents every now and again, and they don't turn down a check when they get in a financial bind, but we're not close. Lylah lives nearby though, and we see each other at least once a week." His face brightened as he talked about his sister.

"That's too bad about your parents," Abigail said, lost for what else to say. Then she faced him, extending her hand to shake his. "Well, Jack, it's great to finally meet you."

"It's equally nice to meet you, Cricket," he said, taking her hand in his. She hoped he didn't notice the way her pulse quickened at his touch.

"Abby," she finally said. "My close friends and family call me Abby."

"It's nice to meet you, Abby." He spoke her name with soft reverence and let his hand linger in hers. This time she feared she may have visibly shivered. With his free hand, Storm reached up and tucked a strand of her hair behind her ear.

"You're really beautiful, Abby," he told her. She tensed, pressing her lips together in a tight, thin line.

"Hey, can't a guy pay you a compliment?"

"As long as that guy knows it's not going to get him anywhere," she said, but there was no conviction in her words and they both knew it.

He cradled her face in his hands, eyes boring into hers, daring her to stop him. Her lips parted as she felt her resolve fade. When he traced her lips with his thumb, she gasped softly. Storm leaned in, brushing his lips across her ear. "Is this off limits?" he asked. She didn't answer. Instead, she closed her eyes and tried to ignore the hitch in her breathing and the steady pounding of her heartbeat.

He dipped his head lower, softly dragging his lips across her cheek. "How about this?"

She felt herself grow hot with desire. "Storm…"

"Jack, remember."

"Jack." Her voice cracked with emotion.

"Abby?" His smile was roguish, and she realized he was taunting her—daring her.

"Don't we have an interview to get to?" she said, drawing from the dwindling well of her resolve and managing to push him away.

"Yes, you're right," he sighed. "But I may need to take *another* cold shower before we go."

Abby silently admired Storm's poise from her seat backstage. Leslie Stokes was the epitome of beauty and grace, but she paled in comparison to her guest.

"Now, here's the question we've all been dying to hear the answer to," Leslie said, pausing for dramatic effect and patting her perfectly coiffed hair.

"Lay it on me, Leslie," Storm said good-naturedly. He seemed at ease, as if he were actually enjoying himself. He sat in a relaxed position; his outstretched legs crossed at the ankles.

"Okay, Storm, tell us, who is this woman who seems to have captured your attention? And more importantly, what does she have that the rest of us don't?"

Leslie winked at the audience and Storm chuckled, a deep, throaty laugh, and slapped his knee. From backstage, Abby held her breath and leaned in closer to the monitors. She knew this was all an act, but she was still anxious to hear his response.

"Well, Leslie, her name is Abigail. At first, she was just a friend, but now…" He broke off, staring into the distance as if deep in thought.

"Now?" Leslie prodded.

He grinned, keeping the audience in suspense for a moment longer. "Now, I'd like to think we're so much more than that. I'm not sure where it's going to lead, but I can honestly tell you she's the first girl who's actually made me think about settling down."

The audience gasped, then cheered.

Abby gasped louder and her cheeks warmed. His demeanor seemed genuine, which was confusing to her. It made her think perhaps she couldn't tell when he was acting after all, and the realization made her physically ill.

"In fact," Storm continued, "I'd love for all of you to meet her in-person. Would you all like that? She's waiting for me backstage. Abby, want to come out here?" The crowd started to holler and applaud, and it took Abby a moment to realize she was being summoned. Panicking, she looked around for the nearest exit but was stopped by a stagehand before she had the chance.

"This way ma'am." The mountain of a man pointed her in the direction of the stage.

She closed her eyes and took two deep, cleansing breaths before she stepped through the curtain. She smiled and waved to the studio audience as she crossed the platform and took a seat in the cream, wingback chair next to Storm's. His eyes followed her movements and she held his gaze, expecting a look of apology but his expression only reflected amusement.

Tech support worked quickly to hook up her microphone as the crowd continued to applaud and Abby waived.

"Well, Abigail," Leslie crooned. "I think I speak for everyone in the studio audience when I say that we are just grateful to have you with us today."

"Thank you so much, Leslie," Abby said, doing her best to match Storm's confident posture and casual speech pattern. "It's so great to be here today." This prompted another loud applause from the crowd.

When the audience quieted down, Leslie continued. "So, Abigail, tell us about Storm."

Abby smiled sweetly, glancing over at Storm and resting her hand on his knee. "Well, there's so much to tell, but I think I'll keep most of that private." She addressed the full room as she spoke, taking on a conspiratorial tone. *What was wrong with her?* She felt like she was pandering, but it was coming so easily to her. "But what I will say, Leslie, is that Storm is one of the sweetest, most generous men I've ever met. I know he's got a bit of a reputation…" She exchanged a knowing glance with the captivated audience, then continued. "But it hasn't scared me off yet." She gave his knee a squeeze and put a little force behind it to make it clear to him that he was in big trouble when all of this was over.

Most of the remaining questions were directed at Storm, but Abby easily fielded any tossed in her direction.

"Well, ladies and gentlemen, I think that's all we have time for on our show today. Storm, Abigail, it was such a pleasure speaking with you both. We hope to see a great deal more of you two in the future," Leslie said in her sing-song voice.

"You can count on it," Storm told her, shaking her hand, then pressing it to his lips. Abby wanted to roll her eyes, but she kept her gaze leveled at Storm and maintained her sickeningly sweet smile.

When they reached backstage, Storm started to speak, but Abby waved him off and rushed for the emergency exit. Throwing open the door, she headed for the nearest bush, vomiting up her breakfast as the alarm bells rang behind her.

Storm rushed after her, followed by two security guards, who he politely dismissed. They went back inside, resetting the alarm.

Abby sat on the curb and put her head between her knees. Storm sat down beside her. "What just happened in there?" he asked.

"Sorry, was it that bad?" She looked up and smiled meekly. "I've never done an interview like that before."

"No, are you kidding me? I meant you were fantastic!"

"Really? I was prepared to murder you when you suggested that I go on stage, but I decided to just follow your lead. I hope I didn't lay it on too thick."

Storm tilted his head to the side, staring at her. His eyes twinkled in amusement, crinkling in the corners. "So, are you telling me that was all an act?" His mouth curved into a challenging grin.

"No more than your, 'ooh, she's so special to me' act," she teased, but it pained her a little to admit aloud she knew his sentiments weren't real.

His expression grew more serious. "Who said it was an act?" But before she could respond, he laughed and reached out his hands, pulling her to her feet. "Let's go, Cricket."

"It's about to start," Abby shouted over her shoulder. She was curled up on the corner recliner, her legs tucked beneath her; arm propped on the edge of the chair as she rested her chin in her hand. Storm came into the living room area wearing sweats and a t-shirt and carrying two bowls of popcorn. He handed one to her, then stretched out on the couch to watch the playback of their interview.

He glanced in Abby's direction, noticing how nervous and attractive she looked as she waited to see herself being interviewed on T.V. for the first time. She'd changed into jeans and a button-up blouse but somehow managed to look more elegant than she had earlier wearing a designer dress and high heels.

When the program started, she sat up straighter. They were calling the segment "Storm Tracker." *Oh, good Lord*, she thought, *is there no end to the banal use of his name?*

"Earlier today I talked with today's hottest couple. Move over Branjelina and Tom-Kat, you had your time in the sun. America now has Stormy Gail," the voiceover announced dramatically.

"Stormy *Gale?*" Abby asked.

"*Gail.* You know. Storm. Abi-*gail.*" He chuckled aloud. "Clever."

"Hmm, clever, or embarrassingly corny?" But her eyes brightened in amusement.

Her cellphone started vibrating, but she ignored it, figuring it was a concerned or enthusiastic family member. She had no idea what she could or should tell them at that point.

Storm's interview was a masterpiece. Abby squirmed in her seat when he began to tell the cameras how he felt about her. Knowing it was all for publicity, the words were like tiny pinpricks to her heart.

When the segment was over and Storm had turned off the T.V., Abby picked up her phone to find out who had been blowing it up with text messages. She groaned as she scrolled through her texts. "My friend Kelly is super persistent," she complained.

"Call her."

"And say what, exactly?"

Storm shrugged. "Tell her whatever you feel comfortable with. Actually, on second thought, hand me your phone."

"What? You can't be serious."

"Of course I'm serious. Hand it over."

Abby laughed, then tossed him her cell. "What are you going to do?"

With a mischievous grin, he began to respond back to Kelly's numerous texts. His thumbs flew across the keypad as his eyes glowed with amusement.

"Storm, seriously, what are you writing?" She was getting worried.

Still grinning, he hit the send button, then tossed the phone back to her.

Abby read the message, then shot him a disapproving glare, though she failed to stifle her laughter as she read it aloud.

I'm shacked up with Storm Jackson and we're having mind-blowing sex as long as he'll have me. Really, his stamina is exhausting.

"You're very naughty," she scolded.

He chuckled, unashamed.

Kelly texted back almost immediately.

Girl, you are blowing up on social media. You must tell me everything.

"Uh oh, apparently I'm famous in the social media realm."

"Um, yeah. Have been since day one outside the hotel."

"Seriously?" Abby squeaked. "What are people saying? Wait a minute, you have social media. What have *you* been saying?"

"Hey," he said, putting up his hands in surrender, "You know I have people who manage my pages. I'm just a pawn in this, same as you."

She thought about taking a peek, then decided against it. Instead, she plopped herself on the couch next to Storm, took a quick selfie of the two of them, then fired it off to Kelly.

"I figure I'll control my own social media content," she explained with a grin.

"Love-crazed fan," he teased.

"You know it." Then she planted a chaste kiss on his cheek and wondered if he knew just how close to accurate his statement was.

"That whole part was true you know?" he said after a moment of silence lapsed between them.

"What part?" she asked, feigning indifference as her cellphone started to vibrate again. This time she picked it up and put it on silent.

"What I said in the interview about you and me." He rose from the couch and pulled her to her feet.

"Storm, it's fine. You don't have to pretend with me."

He leaned in closer. "I'd like to find out where this is going." As he spoke, his lips brushed across her cheek.

"Storm," she pleaded, putting her hands on his chest to keep him at a distance.

"Abby, you think too much," he said, nibbling on her earlobe and pulling her in closer.

She was going to protest again but decided against it. "Oh, screw it," she found herself saying instead. Then her lips found his, taking him by surprise.

A wanting like he'd never experienced consumed him, and he found himself deepening the kiss as he wove his fingers through her silky, honey-blonde hair. "Aww, Abby. Do you have any idea what you do to me?"

Abby's body tingled all over as she considered if it was even half of what he was doing to her, she might have some idea. The voice that typically screamed out in her head when she was making a poor decision was reduced to merely a whisper. A dull whimper. She knew this decision would probably take years to recover from, a lifetime even, but at that moment she didn't care. She knew in her heart he'd be worth it.

"Take me to your room," she said breathlessly.

"Yes ma'am," he obliged, scooping her into his arms and heading towards his bedroom.

He made his way to the bed and playfully plopped her onto it. He bent down and kissed the top of her head, then stepped back for a moment to study her. "Are you sure about this?"

"I've never been so sure and unsure about anything in my life," she confessed. He wasn't certain what to make of her comment, so he remained where he stood.

"I want you," she said.

It was all the prodding he needed. In a flash, he removed his shirt and tossed it in the corner. He leaned over Abby, unbuttoning her blouse so her breasts were exposed. Gently, he kissed each mouthwatering mound. Her breasts were soft, yet supple. It had been awhile since he'd been with someone who hadn't been altered by surgery. He felt himself quiver as if experiencing intimacy for the first time.

Abby's chest rose and fell in anticipation. Instinctively, her hands went to his waistline. She tugged at the waistband of his sweatpants and was surprised to discover he was naked underneath them.

Storm pulled down his sweats, kicking out of them before moving on to Abby's pants. He reached his hands around her waistline, unzipping her jeans and tugging them over her hips. She laid down flat on the bed and let him finish undressing her.

When he stretched his toned, naked body over hers, Abby waited for her inside voice to protest, but it had grown irresponsibly silent.

With a firm, gentle hand, Storm stroked her soft skin. She closed her eyes and let him explore her every curve. With her hair splayed across the pillow, and her lips parted with desire, she was the most beautiful thing he'd ever seen. Her hips arched toward him and she held the sheets beneath her in her fists as she murmured his name. When he slid inside her, she wrapped her arms and legs around him. Without realizing it, her nails dug into his backside as she pulled him closer.

Storm's mouth claimed her throat, then her lips. As he began to move inside her, he matched her rhythm, felt it build at a maddening pace.

"Abby, you've captivated me," he whispered as his teeth grazed her earlobe.

Any bouts of insecurity she'd had about his past lovers were chased away by his well-placed kisses and the longing in his eyes she could tell was only for her.

"Don't stop," she whispered back, hoping she wouldn't wake to find this was all a dream. Between her thighs, her most gentle place throbbed and begged for more. She marveled at the sensations that flowed through her. Storm's gentle hands and soft kisses were a stark contrast to his deep, unrelenting thrusts.

He took his time with her. She wasn't someone to use and cast aside. He enjoyed every moment, every sensation. She smelled of citrus and soap as opposed to the thick, designer perfumes of the women he was used to. He admired the natural blush of her cheeks—preferring it to the ruse of modesty the Hollywood starlets painted on. Her natural lashes were long, and thick, not glued on or coated with black gel. He studied her beautiful face before dipping his head to nuzzle her neck and whisper the things in her ear he didn't dare say to her during the light of day.

When Abby's moans grew more desperate and the arching of her hips reached a mind-blowing pace, he knew she was getting close. He deepened his thrusts as he felt his control slipping away.

She called out his name once more, then he felt her shudder around his manhood as she reached her peak. With a final, determined thrust he found his own release. He whispered her name and a string of lust-crazed obscenities as he lost himself inside her.

"Did I mention that you're sort of adorable?" he murmured as he lay beside her, completely spent. His body was slick with exertion—hers and his.

"You may have mentioned that before," she said sleepily, but happily. As she drifted off to dream, she came to realize that when it came to the affairs of her heart, there was no turning back.

Storm marveled as he watched her sleep. He lifted a small strand of her hair from her cheek, tucked it behind her ear, and nuzzled his face into her neck. She was lovely, pure, and far too good for him. He kissed her shoulder, let himself stay drunk on her presence for a moment longer, then with an exasperated sigh, he lifted her from his bed.

CHAPTER EIGHT

*W*hen Abby awoke the next morning, she was back in her own room and Storm wasn't beside her. At first, she thought it may have all been a dream, but she could still taste him on her lips. Her body felt warm with the memory of his touch. She had expected to feel regret in the morning light, but the feeling didn't come. She did, however, feel an unexpected wave of loneliness at awaking by herself.

She scrambled out of bed, slipped into a robe, and headed to the shared living area in hopes of finding Storm sipping coffee or rummaging around in the kitchenette for something to eat. Any sign he hadn't just abandoned her. Her disappointment grew once she noticed the closed door to his room and realized he was still sleeping behind it. Alone.

Abby was stunned. She'd fully expected to be cast aside once Storm was bored of her, but she hadn't realized it would be before the next morning. The fact that he'd moved her to her own bed so he didn't have to spend a single night with her was both an insult and a major blow to her ego.

Doing her best to shrug it off, she trudged back to her room to grab a shower. She hoped the piping hot water would mask the sting of betrayal she felt. Lost in thought and self-loathing, she didn't notice when the bathroom door opened and Storm slipped into the room. Wordlessly, he slid into the shower behind her, wrapping his muscular arms around her tiny waist. Abby jerked in surprise and whipped around to face him. The pelting water couldn't hide the tears streaming down her face.

"What's wrong?" he asked, reaching up to wipe a tear from her cheek.

"Nothing. Forget it."

"Abby, I…"

"I said, forget it. You don't owe me any sort of explanation. We both know what last night was."

He stepped back from her as if he'd been slapped. "And what was it?" His glare was glacial and his hands clenched at his sides.

His reaction only further enraged her. He had no right to be angry. "Oh, come on. Do I really have to spell it out? Apparently, I'm like any other silly woman who can't resist your charms. And you, well… well you just can't help yourself, can you?"

Storm spoke softly but rage bubbled beneath the surface of his cool demeanor. "I see that your opinion of me hasn't changed." His eyes flashed a dangerous turquoise, but Abby didn't ease up. She was too angry—maybe more so at herself than him, but she wasn't feeling level-headed enough to make the distinction.

"I'd say your inability to even spend a full night with me made it abundantly clear that my opinion of you is spot on." Her bitter words echoed off the walls of the steamy, enclosed shower.

"Well, I guess you still think you've got me all figured out then." And with that, he stepped out of the shower. He grabbed one of the plush towels from the hook, mumbling to himself as he left her alone with her anguish.

When she finished getting ready and left her room, Abby expected to find the suite empty. Instead, Storm was in his usual place on the couch, sipping his coffee as if nothing had happened. She knew she should apologize to him, but her pride couldn't take another hit.

"You ready to go, Cricket?" he asked, barely looking up from his coffee.

She forced a smile. "I'm ready."

"Great, let's go. We have a pretty full day ahead of us."

She nodded, shocked at how quickly he could switch off his feelings. Perhaps it was because his feelings were never truly authentic. The scene they'd played out moments earlier had simply ended and his performance was through. *Actors.* She scooted towards the door, unable to meet his gaze.

Despite her quick pace, Storm beat her to the door. He placed his palm against it, blocking her exit. As he held her gaze in his, the silence in the room threatened to deafen them both. Then he spoke softly. "I couldn't do it."

"Do what?" she seethed. "Stick around until morning like a man?"

His eyes flickered with remorse. "No. See the look of regret on your face in the morning when you woke up next to me." He didn't wait for her to respond. Instead, he opened the door and swept past her into the hallway.

Abby was dazed by his admission. She trailed down the hallway behind him for a few moments, then picked up her pace to catch up. "Hey," she called out to him. Storm stopped in front of the service elevator. He pushed the button before turning around to face her.

Finally reaching the elevator doors, she glared up at him. "Do you think you're the only one who worries they'll be enough in the sober light of day?"

He didn't answer. When the doors opened, she stepped into the elevator, then yanked him inside with her. As soon as the doors closed, her arms circled his neck and she pulled his head down to kiss him. "I'm sorry you thought I'd be disappointed in being with you," she said, between the muffled kisses she planted on his hesitant lips. His arms remained tense at his sides, but she didn't let go. "I regret nothing," she whispered.

At hearing these words, Storm pulled her into his arms and crushed his lips to hers. He wanted to hold her and never let go. As the elevator made its descent, he felt the walls he'd built come crumbling down and he didn't bother to fight the hold Abby was placing on his heart.

Feeling famished, the pair stopped in at a small diner for breakfast. With its fading paint and partially burned out neon sign, the diner looked to be a bit of a dive. Storm reasoned even if someone recognized him, they'd assume a *big star* wouldn't eat at a place like that. But he wore his ball cap down low just in case. Truth being told, dive diners were his favorite. Two or three runny eggs, greasy sausage patties, and a side of hash. It was like a little bit of heaven.

His efforts to disguise himself proved unnecessary though. The diner was empty save for an elderly couple in the back. The old man looked up when the bell above the door announced new arrivals, but then quickly looked away, disinterested.

Despite her hunger, Abby found herself pushing the food around on her plate with a fork. The weight of last night's decision was pressing down on her. The thought of losing her job. Her heart.

"Spit it out, Abby. I can tell you have something to say." Storm was grinning, but even he couldn't mask the worry in his eyes.

"I'm nervous you'll be angry once I say it," she admitted. She shot him a pleading look, silently begging forgiveness for the words she hadn't yet said.

Storm knew this was coming. Abby might not have personal regrets, but he also knew her job was important to her and their professional arrangement was something she'd intend to see through to the end. Despite the stabbing feeling in his heart, he vowed to himself not to make things harder for her. How he handled himself over the next few minutes would be his greatest performance yet.

"I won't be angry." His eyes remained kind and his smile never wavered. "Promise," he said, as he made a gesture of crossing his heart.

She chewed nervously on her bottom lip. "As much as it pains me to say it…" She took a breath, then said in a rush, "I think we need to take a step back from last night."

He looked across the table at her, the longing simmering in his gaze.

Abby squirmed in her seat. "I mean, you were incredible last night. And I love kissing you."

"Oh, you do, do you?" he interrupted, reaching across the table to caress her hand.

She laughed. "Would you stop charming me and listen for a moment?" she scolded. "We can't let what happened last night get in the way of what we're trying to do here. We need to keep things professional."

His eyes crinkled with wicked amusement. "I kiss a lot of people while keeping true to my profession."

She shook her head, grinning as her heart was simultaneously aching. "You're not making this easy. Can we just agree to keep things professional? We'll turn up the heat for the cameras, but when nobody's looking…" She trailed off, inwardly cursing herself for being so darn responsible. She wasn't sure if she even knew how to behave when it came to having Storm all to herself.

"Are you sure that's what you want?" he challenged, keeping his tone playful despite the impact her words were having.

His roguish grin made Abby's heart do flipflops but she kept her tone firm. "Yes, I'm sure."

"Okay," he said, shrugging casually while being secretly thankful for the years his acting coach had devoted to him. "If you're sure."

He went back to eating his breakfast and appeared completely at ease. Inside he was a mess of longing and regret. Neither of them knew at that moment how much they had in common.

CHAPTER NINE

"You know what I was thinking?" Storm said as the pair rode in the backseat of the limo, headed for their first engagement of the day.

Abby knew what *she* was thinking. It had been two days since she'd announced they should take a step back. Two painful days of wanting to touch him. Wanting to let him take her in his arms and make love to her. She thought of little else.

"What?" she asked, trying to sound upbeat despite mourning the memory of his kisses.

Storm grinned at her. "Forget the schedule." He pulled his copy of their itinerary out of his shirt pocket, crumpled it into a ball, and tossed it on the floor.

Abby's mood brightened. "Um, don't you have that electronic on your phone?" she teased.

"Hey, it's symbolic," he grinned. "But seriously, let's play hooky."

"Really?" She knew she should convince him to stick with his plans. It was the responsible thing to do. But she wasn't feeling particularly responsible at that moment.

"Yes, I'll ask my assistant to reschedule my appearances. What do you think about just hanging out with me today?"

"As friends?" she clarified for good measure, though she knew he could easily convince her to break all the rules.

"Of course," he promised. "Well, unless there's hordes of paparazzi clamoring about, in which case I plan to cover you in kisses. For the cameras of course."

Abby laughed and hoped he didn't notice the blush that crept into her cheeks. She thought back on the day's itinerary. Storm had a haircut and a tux fitting. They were both scheduled to check in with Harry. Nothing major.

"That would be fun," she said decidedly. "If you wanted, we could check out your place. I can help you with some decorating tips if you'd like." She did love to decorate, but she had selfish motives as well. She was dying to see the inside of his home. You could tell a lot about a person by how they lived.

"Hmm, that sounds nice. I'll call Patty and ask her to clear the schedule and arrange a car for us to drive."

Less than an hour later, they had traded the limo and driver for a luxury convertible and were driving across town, headed for Storm's home. He lived in an exclusive, but less well-known gated community outside of Beverly Hills. The guard at the gate recognized Storm immediately and waved them through. If he noticed Abby in the seat beside him, he didn't let on.

Abby wasn't sure what to expect, but when she walked through the double wooden doors of his home, what she didn't expect was to be pleasantly surprised by its charm. A large foyer opened into an impressive Great Room. Despite the modern-style spiral chandeliers, light-colored furnishings, and marbled tile that might otherwise feel cold and impersonal, the well-placed décor and panoramic views made his home feel inviting. "You were being modest," she told him. "Your place is incredible. I don't think you need my help with decorating."

When she rounded the corner, she was bowled over by a massive yellow Labrador with brown, wideset eyes and a tongue that hung halfway out of his smiling mouth. She squealed with delight as the overzealous yet gentle brute covered her with sloppy kisses, his tail thumping loudly on the sleek flooring.

"You okay?" Storm asked, laughing and helping her to her feet.

"Oh yes, he seems harmless." Eyes shining with amusement, she wiped the slobber from her cheek. "His name doesn't happen to be Chester, does it?"

"No, it's Max, actually. Why?"

"Oh, no reason," she said, unable to contain her glee as she scratched the dog behind the ears. "I've just always wanted a yellow Lab. My plan was to call him Chester."

"Why don't you get one?"

"I planned to when I first moved in. That's one of the reasons I bought a house with a fenced-in backyard. But it wouldn't be fair to a dog at this point in my life. I work long hours and I'm afraid the dog would either be cooped up in my small house or have to spend a considerable amount of time at doggy daycare. When things slow down, I'll get one." Even as she explained, Abby wondered at what point she ever expected things to slow down for her.

Just then a pretty, young woman with ash-blonde hair came bounding around the corner. "I'm so sorry," she said. "I was on the phone and Max darted off before I could grab him." Abby stared at her, trying her best to contain her jealousy as the woman bent down to ruffle the dog's fur and placed a kiss on his nose. Abby was shocked at her own jealousy—it wasn't her typical nature. But this girl couldn't be older than twenty. She knew Storm's dog, used his phone, and hung out even while he was away. Who was she?

"Abigail, this is my assistant, Patty. Patty, this is Abigail."

Abby felt a wave of relief. She extended her hand to Patty. "So nice to meet you."

"Likewise," the assistant said, then turned her attention to Storm. "I've managed to move all of your appointments. I emailed you a revised itinerary for the week. I'm going to take Max to the groomer for a bath and a nail trim, then back to my place, if that works for you."

"Yes, thank you Patty. And thanks again for taking care of Max while I'm away. I knew he'd be lonely."

"Anytime." Her eyes sparkled at Storm's praise. "It was nice to meet you, Abigail," she said.

Storm knelt down next to his dog, "I miss you ole' boy. Be good for Patty." Then, in a flurry of activity, Patty and the dog were gone.

"She likes you," Abby wanted to tell Storm. It was obvious, the way Patty flittered and fussed about. But Abby thought better of telling him. It might make the working relationship strained—or make things awkward for Patty. "She seemed nice," she said instead.

"Patty is a lifesaver. Harry hired her on as a part-time intern, but I stole her away from him. I figure Harry gets ten percent of my earnings, which is highway robbery, so my stealing staff from him sort of evened things out." Storm was grinning, clearly pleased with himself and not at all offended at the chunk of change Harry was costing him.

After a light lunch at Storm's (prearranged by one of the housekeeping staff so Storm merely had to pop it in the oven for thirty minutes), he and Abby enjoyed a glass of rosé from his veranda that overlooked a private beach.

"This is amazing," she mused, closing her eyes as the breeze caressed her face and the sweet liquid swept across her tongue.

Storm smiled over at her, amazed at the pleasure she found in the smallest of things. "California wines are amongst the best in the world."

She enjoyed wine but didn't know enough about it to agree or disagree. She nodded instead.

"Let's go for a walk," he offered, holding out his hand to her.

She glanced over at him, questioning whether his gesture was too intimate, but she took his hand and allowed herself to be led outside. Within the gated community, she felt safe from the wandering eyes and invasive cameras of the press.

The pair strolled along the sidewalk in comfortable silence, hands intertwined. The sky above them was a perfect shade of blue. The heat from the brilliant California sun was tempered behind fluffy, cotton clouds. Abby reminded herself to keep things professional, but then overrode that voice, partially convincing herself she was doing this as part of the act and that pretending to be Storm's girlfriend in public was indeed, her job.

"Storm," a woman's husky voice shouted from behind them, interrupting Abby's thoughts and the tranquility of the moment. "Storm," the voice repeated, more forcefully.

Storm whipped his head around, then grinned, calling out to the woman. "Victoria, you beautiful vixen, come here."

A woman wearing a floral, black and white dress that flared above the knees came sashaying down the street, walking a miniature poodle. She placed a slender, manicured hand on Storm's shoulder and leaned in to kiss his cheek.

"Victoria, darlin', this is Abigail," Storm introduced. Dropping Abby's hand, he reached up to give Victoria's gorgeous dark locks a flirty tug.

Victoria's smile faded as she seemed to notice Abby for the first time. "Hello, there," she said smoothly. Her tone was polished, but cool.

Abby smiled coolly back. She wasn't paid to make nice with the other women in Storm's life.

"Haven't seen you around lately," Victoria said, her red lips pulled into a pout as she returned her attention to Storm.

"Oh, sweetheart, sorry, I've been a bit busy promoting the upcoming film. What about you? Any movie prospects lately?"

Victoria shook her head *no*, her lips still formed into a pout.

Abby didn't recognize the woman and figured she must be an upcoming actress that hadn't made it yet. Then again, she lived in a ritzy neighborhood for a struggling actress. Perhaps she already came from money

With a seductive grin, Storm said, "Well, I'll put in a good word for you with Harry." His comment seemed to please Victoria because her eyes lit up and her pout was replaced by a warm smile.

"Listen doll, we've got to get going. Don't be a stranger, though." Storm made a production of taking the woman by the hand, turning her palm upward, and planting a soft kiss on her wrist. He winked, waved goodbye to her, then slung an arm around Abby's shoulders and led her back to his house. If he noticed she'd grown quiet, he didn't mention it.

"What was all of that about?" Abby finally asked once they were behind closed doors.

"What do you mean?" Storm blinked in confusion.

"I mean all of that. The flirting. The phony charm."

"Are you talking about Victoria? What, are you jealous?" His face split into a wide grin.

"No, I'm not jealous," she defended. "I just don't understand why you can't just be yourself?"

Storm's eyebrows furrowed. The smile remained on his face, but it didn't reach his eyes. "I'm afraid you'd find the real me disappointing." Despite his smile, his tone was somber.

Abby's green eyes widened in surprise at seeing his troubled face. Her accusing tone softened to one of wonder. "Why would you think that?"

"Think about it, Abby. In the movies I'm coached on every move I make; handed every line. Of course, it's easy for people to think I'm smooth and sexy. And in real life, people have those same expectations. They want to see the character they think they fell in love with on the screen."

"Well, I've seen the real you and I like it best."

He narrowed his eyes, challenging her. "How do you know that's not just another act?"

"Because I know you," she said. Her voice was nearly a whisper and her eyes bore into his, daring him to refute her statement.

Storm stepped toward her, then stopped himself. He wanted to respect her wishes to keep things professional. But beyond that, he could see in her eyes the person she thought he was and he wasn't sure he could measure up. He couldn't bear the thought of disappointing her. He suspected neither his ego nor his heart could take it.

He frowned in her direction, eyes clouding with uncertainty. Then, without warning, his expression changed and amusement flickered across his handsome face. "Let's go out and have some fun tonight."

Before Abby's eyes, the broody, volatile male disappeared and was replaced by confident, boyish charm. Both personas were equally a genuine part of who he was, she surmised.

"I'd like that," she found herself agreeing.

They went dancing at an obscure nightclub on the outside of town. It wasn't fancy. Some might even call it seedy. There were no red velvet ropes or bouncers denying entrance to those who weren't blessed with wealth or beauty. The pair found an empty booth in the back where they enjoyed an overabundance of drinks from the shadows and a few turns on the dance floor. Storm was a terrific dancer, but Abby could hold her own. The music pumped through them as their bodies moved in unison to the beat. Abby had an image of them making love, how in sync everything had felt, but she pushed the unwelcome, albeit fond memory away.

Throughout the evening they noticed a few nightclub patrons whisper and point in their direction, but nobody bothered them. Abby suspected the poor lighting of the club made it impossible for people to know for sure if the gorgeous man they were seeing on the dancefloor was indeed the famous Storm Jackson, so they kept their distance.

"You're an amazing dancer," Storm told her as they slid exhausted back into their booth. His words were slurred a bit and Abby realized neither of them were in any position to drive.

"I'll call Patty," Storm said, as if reading her thoughts.

Despite the late hour and short notice, Patty came. She drove them back to Storm's home rather than the hotel. She must have figured their inebriated condition wouldn't do for the new image Storm was trying to build. Or rather, the studio was. Patty knew enough about her employer to know he rarely cared what others thought of him.

Abby was in better shape than Storm, so she and Patty helped him up the front steps and onto the couch. "You can take the master bedroom," Patty told Abby.

"You sure? Are you going home?"

"Nah, I'll take the guestroom … stick around to make sure he's okay."

Abby smiled. "You do this for him often?"

Patty laughed. "Only on occasion. Usually Storm's more careful when he goes out drinking. You must be a bad influence on him." She laughed again, but despite Abby's drunken haze she caught a look of sadness in Patty's young eyes. Remembering her suspicion that Storm's assistant had a crush on him, she felt a pang of guilt.

"Shall we take off his shoes?" Patty asked.

The two women removed his shoes, then his socks. Storm's assistant grabbed the blanket draped over the sofa and tucked Storm in.

"He's lucky to have you," Abby noted, and Patty blushed crimson at the unexpected praise.

CHAPTER TEN

"*W*hat's on the agenda tonight, Patty?" Storm asked the next morning. He was lying on the couch, nursing a hangover. Abby on the other hand was showered, dressed, and enjoying a bowl of cereal with Patty. The two women were seated at the breakfast nook that connected to the living room, talking in hushed tones out of respect for Storm's splitting head. Max lay at their feet, tail thumping happily as he chewed noisily on a milk bone.

Patty picked up her tablet and studied Storm's calendar. "Well, you've got the appearance at the new restaurant downtown, then Ryan Tyler's party."

"Ryan Tyler?" Abby spoke up enthusiastically. Clearly, she hadn't studied the schedule very well. "From the series, *Passion Alley*?"

"Cancel it," Storm told Patty without answering Abby.

"The restaurant appearance or the party?"

"The party."

His assistant pursed her lips. "But you RSVP'd," she reminded him with a whine.

"Just make an excuse for me, okay doll?" He popped the aspirin Patty had left for him on the sofa table, then cradled his head in his hands.

"Yes, sir." She swept up her stylus and tapped it feverishly on the screen, furrowing her brow in concentration. "It's done," she announced, looking up from her screen and smiling broadly as if completing his request was the best part of her day. She practically skipped as she lifted the empty cereal bowls from the table and headed towards the kitchen.

Once they were alone, Abby eyed Storm. "I get it, you don't want to go with me as your girlfriend because you don't think your friends will believe you'd actually be dating me." She tried to keep her voice neutral. Her face was impassive.

Storm glanced up at her. "No, I just don't feel up to it," he said with a shrug.

"No, it's a good idea. We've come too far to have our cover blown."

Storm opened his mouth to say something but closed it again. "What should we do instead?" he asked.

After Storm was up and showered Abby made an excuse to go into work for a few hours. She needed to get her thoughts and feelings in order. Patty offered to stick around, make Storm some soup, and nurse him into a presentable state for that evening's restaurant appearance.

First order of business was to check in with Tammie and convince her that, while things were going well, she was keeping her wits about her. The latter part couldn't be further from the truth but she was learning to be a better actress.

"There's a considerable pay raise in your future if you can pull this one off," Tammie told her.

Next, she checked in with her assistant.

"Katerina is taking great care of all of your other clients," her assistant assured her cheerily.

"I'll just bet she is." Abby didn't bother to keep the irritation out of her tone.

She returned a half a dozen emails before calling it quits for the day. She headed to her place to get ready for the evening from the privacy of her own bedroom.

When Storm picked her up in the limo, and she came out of the house in a strappy little number that left him reeling, he told her she looked beautiful. When he leaned in to kiss her, she turned her head and offered him her cheek. He took the rejection in stride, smiling as he held open the car door for her.

Despite her cool demeanor in the limo, Abby handled the restaurant crowd with grace and sophistication. She and Storm split an appetizer and engaged in playful banter as patrons gawked and cameras flashed. But Storm noticed she'd been acting differently since that morning when he turned down the invitation to Ryan Tyler's party. It bothered her. He could tell.

With the obligatory appearance behind him, and the limo rounding the final corner back to their hotel suite, he couldn't stand her indifference any longer.

"You've been sort of quiet all day," he noted.

"Have I?" She hadn't, really. At least she'd tried not to. "Sorry," she continued. "I guess my mind has been wandering, thinking about all the stuff I need to catch up on at home and at work." She smiled over at him, but he knew she wasn't telling him the full truth. She actually believed he hadn't wanted to take her to the party because he felt she was beneath him. As he stared at her innocent face, he thought how nothing could be further from the truth.

"Abby?"

"Yeah?" She sounded far away.

"I didn't take you to Ryan Tyler's party because he's pretty wild. I didn't want you to see that lifestyle—the drugs, the women. You're too good for that. I didn't want to give you the impression that's who I am."

He stared out the window as he spoke, uncomfortable sharing his feelings so openly.

When he looked over at her, her green eyes glistened with tears.

"I'm sorry," he said, "I didn't mean to make you cry."

Embarrassed and furious with herself for allowing her emotions to get the better of her, she wiped her tears with the back of her hand. "No, it's fine," she said. But she didn't scoot closer to him. Instead, she returned her hands to her lap. She wanted to believe him. She wanted to curl up in his lap and let him whisper all the pretty words he'd told her when they'd made love and that she was so desperate to hear again. She wanted to pretend she wasn't gullible and accept all the lovely flatteries that flowed from his beautiful mouth. But he'd admitted it before. He'd been coached on the right things to say. The right ways to act. She shouldn't be angry. He couldn't help himself. If anything, she was to blame for being naïve enough to think she would be immune to it all.

When they reached the hotel suite, Abby mumbled something about turning in early and headed toward her room.

"Can we talk about this?" Storm asked.

She offered him a tight smile. "Everything's fine. Really, there's nothing to talk about." She tried to side-step him, but he positioned himself in front of her, blocking the door to her room.

"Cut it out," he said, his eyes flashing in anger. "You know what I told you in the limo is true. I'm not that guy from the tabloids. I'm not just feeding you lines and there's no way in hell I could ever be ashamed of you. You said it before, you know me." He grasped both of her hands in his and pulled her toward him as his eyes burned into hers.

"You know me," he said softly but with more urgency. He leaned in and kissed her cheek. She closed her eyes, for but a moment, then opened them again to stare into his.

Storm's blue-green eyes held a sea of emotion. "I like you Abby," he confessed. "I like you a lot."

His lips caressed her chin, then her cheek. She sighed, despite herself. Storm's gaze conveyed a passion and vulnerability no acting coach could teach. At least, Abby hoped they couldn't.

"I want you, Abby," he whispered. "I need you so bad."

She'd heard these words more times than she could count; the first time being from the lying lips of her high school boyfriend when he tried (unsuccessfully, to her everlasting satisfaction) to convince her that losing her virginity in the backseat of a dirty pickup truck was the ultimate romantic experience. These lines typically had no impact on her. They were usually followed by *you're so beautiful*, or *I think I love you*—hollow utterances that resulted in an early end to the evening.

She didn't have time for games. But tonight, listening to Storm whisper these same words to her, hearing the sincerity in his voice, seeing the yearning in his eyes, the words were having a powerful impact.

Storm's warm lips landed on hers. The heat of his breath, of his body, made her dizzy with excitement and need. As her resolve faded, replaced by desire, Abby thought if he didn't put an end to her misery, she might combust.

His own need was evident. She could feel his hardness and desperation when he pressed against her. Giving in, she whispered back, "I believe you." She stood on her tiptoes and lengthened the kiss. "I want you too, Storm."

"You absolutely sure this time?" he asked as his lips roved over hers.

All Abby could do was nod. Her throat was raw with emotion. She let her lips trail down his neck and heard the growl of his desire. His hands fisted in her hair and she gasped when his lips once again met hers.

Storm pulled away for a moment, placing his hands on her shoulders and looking her square in the eye. "If we do this, there's no second guessing this time. No regrets."

Abby nodded once more.

"Say it, Abby."

"No regrets," she said hoarsely.

They were the only words he needed to hear. He held nothing back, deepening the kiss while stripping off his clothes where they stood. He moved on to undressing Abby, letting her clothes drop to the floor. He wanted to take her right there on the sofa, or on the floor. He lifted her in his arms instead and made his way to her bedroom.

"This will put us more on your terms," he told her as he laid her on her bed.

An uneasy look flickered across her face.

"I won't leave you this time. I'll stay, I promise," he told her as earnestly as he could.

"Okay," she said, visibly relaxing despite her growing desire.

He covered her in kisses, nibbling on her ear and whispering the things he wanted to do to her. Abby returned his affections, kissing his chest and running her tongue down his torso. She no longer cared how much more experienced he was than her. He wanted her—that's all that mattered at the moment; all that she needed for her confidence to be restored.

Storm wanted to ask again if she was sure, but he was afraid she would change her mind.

"Please, make love to me," she whispered, easing his worries.

Abby allowed herself to relax as Storm pleasured her with his hands and his mouth. She reached for him, coaxing him closer as he covered her body with his. He entered her slowly, his fingers trembling. He felt like a teenager—excited and unsure. Abby both steadied him and put him on edge. She moaned softly, rocking her hips upward to invite him in. Her delicate fingers trailed down his back as she matched his rhythm with her own.

She bit down on her lip to keep from telling Storm all the things she wished she could say. She was crazy about him. He made her crazy—in every way possible. She rejoiced in his warmth and virility as he took her higher and higher. "Storm!" she finally cried out as she peaked. He climaxed inside her, whispering her name over and over as she clung to him.

Beads of sweat covered Abby's forehead and Storm brushed the damp hair out of her eyes with his fingertips. She smiled and managed a contented sigh as he pulled her close, spooning her body with his. "No regrets," he said again, and she nodded in full agreement. He kissed the back of her neck, and before long was snoring softly.

CHAPTER ELEVEN

*S*torm lay in bed, watching Abby sleep, admiring the rise and fall of her chest. With the morning sunrays playing across her face, she looked serene. When he planted a soft kiss on her shoulder, she stirred. Her eyes fluttered open and she smiled up at him.

"Good morning," he crooned, studying her face. He was pleased to observe she looked shy, but not at all remorseful.

"Good morning." Bleary eyed, she extended her body in a catlike stretch. "What are you doing?" she asked sleepily.

"Watching you sleep." He grinned. "And now that I say it out loud, I realize how creepy it sounds."

She laughed and rewarded him with a peck on the cheek.

"I had a great time last night," he said, choosing his words carefully. *You were wonderful*, or *that was so hot*, while true, might be perceived as comparisons to past lovers.

"Mmm…. me too."

"Now, if you don't mind, I've needed to take a leak for the past hour," he said, rolling out of bed.

"Well, this moment is now ruined," she laughed. "Why didn't you get up and go?"

"I promised I'd be here when you woke up. I take my promises very seriously," he said, only half joking.

Abby rolled her eyes. "Now you're being dramatic."

"I'm an actor darling, we're always dramatic." He planted a kiss on her nose. Brushing the hair from her eyes with his hands, he said, "I just didn't want you to think I'd bailed." Then he bent down and kissed her smartly on the mouth before heading for the bathroom. When Abby heard the shower running moments later, she resisted the urge to join him.

Dressed and showered, Abby emerged from her room to find Storm setting out breakfast in the dining area. He must have ordered room service. She watched him from the doorway, admiring the way he carefully set out each plate. Her mouth began to water but she suspected it was more from the way he looked—shirtless in jeans and bare feet—than from how the food smelled.

"I see we still can't afford a shirt," she teased.

A knock at the door interrupted her thoughts. Storm opened the door to their suite and invited the visitor in. Abby recognized her as the young lady from the front desk. Her name was Indiah. A pretty name. Pretty girl, really. Soft, brown eyes that held a glint of mischief. Her thick, caramel-colored hair was pulled back into a loose hairband and small wisps of hair hovered across her forehead.

Abby found herself studying Indiah's delicate features as she wondered what the obviously starstruck girl was doing in Storm's suite.

Storm, on the other hand, didn't appear to find it the least bit peculiar and Abby smiled to herself, amused he was either oblivious to how women grasped at any excuse to catch a glimpse of him—or so used to it that it no longer registered as odd.

Wearing her brightest smile, Indiah handed Storm an envelope, performed a small curtsy (to which Abby stifled a laugh at the girl's over-the-top antics), then politely excused herself.

Storm opened the envelope and removed an invitation. As he read it, he smiled, then motioned Abby over. "We've been invited to a co-ed baby shower this weekend," he explained.

"Both of us?" She playfully snatched the card from his hand, certain he was kidding. The invitation looked expensive. Pale bluish-gray elephants covered the front. The information was professionally embossed in silver.

Help us welcome baby Cobalt.

Abby read the invitation aloud, then waved it in the air. "Cobalt?" she said laughing. "What kind of a name is that? Why must all of you Hollywood-types choose the most off-the-wall, obscure names?"

"Hey, why you gotta paint us all with the same brush?" he laughed, throwing up his hands.

"Oh, I'm sorry *Storm*, does that not apply to you?"

CHAPTER TWELVE

*A*fter more than a week of rearranging her life for Storm's schedule, Abby decided it was time for him to make some adjustments of his own. Yes, he'd cleared one day for her, but it was still to do things his way. She needed at least one day on her terms.

"What's on your mind?" he asked as he stretched out on the couch to enjoy his morning cup of coffee.

"I need to fit a few things into your schedule over the next couple days."

"Fair enough," he obliged, admiring the way Abby's damp hair clung to her clothes and trying to keep the lust out of his eyes.

She sat down on the couch beside him and picked up the hotel notepad. She scribbled on the paper, then paused to chew on her pen, her brow furrowed in thought. She jotted down a couple more things, tore the piece of paper from the pad and handed it to Storm. Her lips quivered in the corners as she tried not to smile.

He read it over, nodding. "Checking in at your work. Okay. Drinks with some of your friends. Okay, I'll bite." Then he paused and cleared his throat uncomfortably. "Um, breakfast at your parents' tomorrow?"

"It's a family tradition. Second Sunday of every month." She was trying hard to suppress her laughter.

"Okay, I can do that," he said, sounding doubtful, even as he said it.

"Relax, that one was more of a joke. I can let you off the hook. I am certain you can manage to stay out of trouble for a few hours without me."

"Don't count on it, Cricket," he laughed, visibly relaxing.

"But would breakfast be so bad?" she asked, casting him a sheepish look that told him she really wanted him to go with her.

"Parents don't like me," he said firmly. But even as he said it, he found himself giving in.

On the way to Abby's parents' house, Storm shifted in his seat, readjusting it several times.

"You're nervous," she observed.

"Nah," he said, but his worried grin gave him away.

"Don't be nervous," she said, patting his leg. She let her hand rest on his thigh a moment longer than she should have, then retracted it.

"I can't believe we've already made it to the *meet the parents* stage in our relationship," Storm joked. "Just over a week ago, you couldn't stand me. You do move fast!"

Abby couldn't help but laugh. "What can I say?" she teased. "You're like wine. An acquired taste."

"Hmm, and not everyone acquires it," he laughed in response. He wanted to tell her she was also like wine. Intoxicating, with a tendency to go straight to his head.

"Pull over," Storm said, breaking the comfortable silence of their morning drive.

Abby glanced over and saw a woman on the side of the road, hood up and leaning under it. The woman appeared to be in her mid-fifties. A little heavy set, but attractive.

Impressed Storm even took notice, she pulled to the side of the road. Her car had barely come to a complete stop before he was out if it, crossing to where the lady was and offering her a hand. Abby watched from the car as he fiddled with the wires under the hood, all the while chatting the lady up. The woman seemed grateful, pleased with the help; but if she recognized Storm, she didn't let on.

He motioned over to Abby, and from what she could gather from his game of charades, he intended to jump-start the woman's car and needed her to position her car accordingly. Hoping this good deed wouldn't be the end of her own car battery, Abby managed to turn her car around on the shoulder, then pulled to the side so her car was facing the stranger's. She proudly got out of her car and opened the trunk to retrieve her jumper cables; something the woman seemed to be without, but Abby's father had insisted she carry around.

On a mission not to be upstaged by Storm, she popped the hood of her old sedan, hooked the cables to both vehicles, started up her car, then instructed the lady to do the same. Within moments the woman's car fired up and she was back in business. The stranger thanked them both, hugging Abby and offering Storm a friendly handshake before she drove away.

When the pair climbed back into the car, Storm was silent.

"If I didn't know you better, I'd say you're a little miffed that woman didn't recognize you," Abby teased.

Other than a grunt, he met her assessment with stony silence.

Sensing she'd hit a nerve, she eased up. "I'm sure the lady just didn't believe a big movie star would stop to help her with her car trouble; especially one riding shotgun in a beat-up sedan."

He offered a faint smile. "It's strange you know. The way fame works."

When she didn't answer, he continued.

"When I started out, I would have given anything to be recognized. Then once I had a few movies under my belt, suddenly I couldn't walk my dog or go to a grocery store without being hounded by people. When it happens to you, you plead for your privacy; learn to take precautions so people don't recognize you, and long for the days when you were another faceless person in the crowd."

"And now?" she asked after Storm grew quiet.

"Now? Now that I'm in the twilight of my career, I worry about no longer being relevant. I abhor the constant invasion of privacy but fear the day I'm no longer recognized. I guess I'd settle for somewhere in between."

Abby patted his hand. "You are *hardly* in the twilight of your career."

"I have six months left on my contract with the studio. I'm locked into one more movie deal. After that…"

"And how do you feel about that?" she asked, hoping she didn't sound like a therapist.

"Honestly, I'm not sure. My agent is already negotiating my next contract. The success of this next movie will weigh heavily on the final terms. But I'm not sure it's what I want."

Abby's eyes darted from him, to the road, then back to him. She appreciated how he was opening up to her. On the other hand, she knew the importance of first impressions and her parents would be less than thrilled if they arrived late.

"You can get back on the road," he told her, grinning. "I won't fall apart on you."

She put on her blinker and merged back into traffic. She'd given herself enough time that morning to ensure they'd arrive on time, no matter what distractions Storm tried to put in their way.

As they neared the entrance to Trousdale Estates where Abby grew up, she noticed Storm sit up straighter in his seat. A look of bewilderment was etched on his handsome face. "Your parents live here?"

She shrugged. It was her turn to feign modesty. "What, did you think I actually grew up poor?" she said playfully.

"What do they... How did... Wait, is your father Donald Travis, the real estate tycoon?"

"Don't let my mother hear you say that," Abby warned. "Believe me, that woman works tirelessly behind the scenes and is every bit as responsible for their success as my father is."

"Amazing," was all he could say. Here he'd worried he'd made her uncomfortable with the size of his home and she'd grown up in a neighborhood that made his little gated community look like the poor house by comparison. With her own modest home and aging car, he marveled that Abby was a walking contradiction to her upbringing.

When they pulled into the drive, Abby reached over and squeezed his hand. "Relax, it's just brick and mortar. Oh, and two people behind those walls who are prepared to rain down fire if anything happens to their only daughter." And with that, she placed a quick peck on his cheek then stepped smoothly out of the car.

"Mom, Dad, I'd like you to meet Storm Jackson," she said brightly once they were inside. "Storm, these are my parents, Donald and Milly."

Her mother gushed and moved in for a bear hug. Storm politely obliged.

But when her father gave Storm a pointed look and ignored his outstretched hand, Abby realized she may have made a mistake bringing him to meet them.

"Yeah, I know who you are," her dad said with a scowl.

Storm retracted his hand, but without missing a beat said, "Can't believe everything you hear."

"Oh, I think I can quickly assess for myself what sort of person I'm dealing with." Her father glared. Storm stared coolly back.

"Let's take our seats," her mother cooed nervously.

The scene at breakfast was not ideal. Milly was polite and did little to hide that she was a fan. Donald, on the other hand, was less than civil. He grilled Storm on his intentions before he'd taken his seat at the dining room table. There were a few moments of peace while her father said grace, but after that, each time Storm took a bite of food, her dad fired off another condescending question. *Did Storm plan on having a real career some day? Did his contract require him to only play in films that lacked depth?*

Abby was mortified and finally yelled at her father to cut it out. Storm took it in stride, as if it was another run of the mill interview. He was charming, calm, but came across as genuine. Abby wanted to give him a huge kiss for his efforts, but instead she gave his leg a reassuring squeeze from below the table before taking his hand in hers. His palm was a tad damp, the only evidence her father was getting under his skin.

After breakfast, they were ushered to the living room for tea. Abby wandered to the kitchen and found her mother in front of the sink, rinsing dishes.

"What is his problem?" she fumed.

"Well, your father is old-fashioned."

"And?"

"And people who are old-fashioned still like to read the newspaper," she said, one eyebrow raised. Her tone was stern but it didn't mask her amusement.

"Shit," was all Abby managed before covering her mouth and whispering an apology to her mother for the use of profanity. She hadn't considered what her father would think about having the nation know she was shacking up with an actor at some fancy hotel.

"I want details," her mother whispered, gushing. Abby ignored her and rejoined her father and Storm in the living room. She took a seat next to Storm, careful to keep an appropriate distance between them despite her desire to crawl into his lap.

"So, how did you two meet?" her mother asked, entering the room with a tray of tea and freshly baked scones. Abby wondered to herself when her mother learned to bake. And when the heck did her mother get a tea set? Despite her fancy surroundings, Abby's mother was more of a black coffee and chipped novelty mug sort of woman. Something Abby had inherited.

"Well, your daughter kept following me around after press conferences…"

Abby choked on her tea. "He's kidding," she said, regaining her composure. Her father shot her a look. "Dad, he's kidding. We met through work, actually. Me being from a PR firm, it's fairly common to meet celebrities. Storm's studio was using the firm to help publicize his upcoming movie and we just hit it off." *Lies, lies.* Abby couldn't remember the last time she'd so blatantly lied to her parents. Probably not since high school.

"Doesn't your work have strict policies against dating your clients?" Her father was asking her, but he never took his accusing eyes off Storm.

"Usually," Abby started to say, "but…" She was having trouble finding a response. Dating clients was strictly against the rules. The magnitude of that fact was sinking in for the first time.

"Sir, I'm crazy about your daughter. Crazy about her. I wouldn't do anything to jeopardize her job. And neither would Abby. She has a good head on her shoulders."

Abby's mother sighed from her perch on the arm of the sofa. Abby's heart flip-flopped in her chest, but she silently reminded herself this was all part of the act. Disappointment fluttered in her belly, but she reached out to grasp Storm's hand in hers. *Just selling it,* she told herself.

"I'm sorry about my dad," she told Storm as they drove back to the hotel. "I know you were already apprehensive about meeting him." She cast a sheepish glance in his direction.

"Nah, I'm used to it," he said, shrugging his shoulders. "I told you, parents don't like me."

"It's not that. My dad's just...protective."

"And with good reason," Storm teased, edging closer to her. "I'm not to be trusted."

Her heart hammered in her chest. Her heart, she realized, was what she could no longer trust.

CHAPTER THIRTEEN

*F*eeling guilty for the way her family had treated Storm, Abby wanted to do something to make amends. She invited him to dinner at her place, offering to make him a homecooked meal.

"You know I can't resist you or home cooking," he'd told her.

He had lunch plans that day with his sister, so Abby took the opportunity to get things done back at her place. Light housekeeping. Mowing. When she was done, she wandered to the kitchen to survey the contents of her fridge. Realizing she didn't have much to make a proper meal, she decided she'd have to take a trip to the grocery store.

She looked down at her grungy clothes, deciding she'd shower and change once she returned from the store. She traded in her grass-stained sneakers for a pair of flipflops before heading out.

At the store she picked up two T-bone steaks from the butcher, then fresh vegetables for a salad. She caught whispers behind her but she tuned them out. No doubt some young kids were whispering about her fashion choice. But what did she care?

When she rounded the corner in search of the wine aisle, she came face to face with a small mob of people. She smiled but took a step backwards to create some distance. The throng pressed forward, along with their questions. *Are you Storm's girlfriend? Is Storm here? Who is your designer?* Abby figured that last question was laced with sarcasm.

She tried to politely excuse herself and steer her cart around the overzealous group. One of the shoppers rushed forward, slamming into her shopping cart which sent the handle jamming into her ribs. After getting over the initial shock, Abby used the cart as a shield. She leaned into it with full force. People scattered to get out of her way as she maneuvered her cart towards the front entrance. When she reached the double doors, she abandoned her cart of groceries as she mouthed an apology to the nearest cashier.

In the parking lot, she made a beeline to her car. A local news van was pulling into the parking lot but she managed to duck him. Her heart was pounding and her ribs were throbbing as she put her car in gear and raced away from the store. Tonight, she decided, she'd be stuck with takeout and whatever wine she had in her cupboards.

Abby hadn't planned to tell Storm about the encounter at the store, but when the shopping cart injury had her wincing at his bear hug, the secret was already close to coming out. Once he cast her a puzzled look at the takeout boxes, after she'd promised him a homecooked meal, she knew she'd have to come clean.

When she filled him in on the events at the store, she could tell he was infuriated. But he kept his head about him, likely not wanting to spoil their evening.

"How was lunch with Lylah?" she asked in a lame attempt to steer the subject away from her injuries.

Storm grunted. Abby wasn't the only one trying to avoid what transpired while they were apart. He didn't want to tell her lunch with Lylah had been an intervention, with Harry joining them unexpectedly.

"Look," Harry had said, "she seems like a sweet girl but I'm worried about you. You've blown off engagements to spend time alone with her. Shirked responsibilities. It's not like you."

At seeing the smirk on Storm's face, his sister had cut in. "We just don't want to see you get hurt if she turns out to be another gold-diggi…"

Storm had cut the pair of them off. "I think I love her," he'd admitted aloud.

His sister nodded, knowingly. She knew it took a lot for her brother to fall, and she'd recognized the look on his face when he'd talked about Abby during his interview with Leslie Stokes.

"Does she feel the same about you?" she had asked gently.

Storm hadn't responded to her question. He wasn't sure he knew—or wanted to know—the answer.

"Hello?" Abby pressed when Storm continued to stare blankly at her. "How did it go?"

"She warned me about getting too close to you," he finally revealed with a laugh.

"She was right to warn you," Abby said, trying to distract him with a kiss.

Her distraction tactic only worked for a moment. Then Storm pulled back from her. "After what happened to you today, we're getting a bodyguard," he insisted.

"No way. I won't let you go through that extra expense and trouble just for me."

"It's no trouble. Besides, it's a matter of routine when a movie is so close to coming out and the paparazzi are in full force."

"Nice try," she said, laughing. "I don't buy it. I can tell when you're acting."

He grinned. "Good, then you know when I do something like this, that it's real." And without warning, his lips locked with hers and she forgot to protest further.

The local station wasted no time reporting the story. The evening news was playing in the background while Storm and Abby enjoyed boxed brownies and a glass of wine from her couch. When Storm caught her name being thrown about, he glanced up at the television. And there it was, leaked cellphone footage of Abby shopping in a faded t-shirt, threadbare sweats, and navy blue flipflops.

To Storm, she looked as sexy as ever. Of course he was at an advantage. He knew what she looked like underneath those clothes she wore that weren't fit for a yard sale. The comments from the reporter weren't as kind. Storm's eyes darted nervously to Abby's but she was grinning.

"Finally," she said with a laugh. "Finally they've managed to capture my true essence." Then she clinked her glass to his.

Grinning, Storm plucked the remote from the sofa table, switched off the television, and moved in closer to her. Not even the press could ruin this night for them.

CHAPTER FOURTEEN

"*A*re you nervous," Abby asked Storm as they prepared for the press junket showing of *Higher Caliber 3*.

"Nah," he said, shrugging his shoulders.

"Liar," she teased. She squeezed his hand and kissed him on the cheek. "It'll be fantastic."

"How would you know? You haven't even read the script."

"Because you're in it," she told him, no longer caring if she sounded like just another adoring fan. She was an adoring fan, she supposed.

"Thanks for the well-meaning, albeit misplaced confidence." Storm pulled her onto his lap. "We don't have to go, you know. We could stay in. Harry's going, so he can answer any questions at the press conference afterwards."

"And miss the chance to see you squirm as you watch yourself on the big screen?" Abby planted a chaste kiss on his cheek. "Not a chance."

Abby never imagined she'd find herself on a movie date with an actual movie actor. The newly hired bodyguard sat two seats over from them, ready to pounce if needed. Harry and Lylah sat one row back, giving the couple some space.

"I suppose in your line of work you don't ordinarily take your dates to movies?" she asked.

"No, I love the movies." Then he grinned. "I just try to avoid taking a date to one of my own."

"Yes, that might be a bit tacky. And awkward." Then she smiled at him. "Then again, we're here now…"

He laughed and gave her hand a squeeze. What he wanted to do was put his arm around her and kiss her graceful neck but he worried once he started, he couldn't stop there. Sitting so close to her for two hours without kissing her was going to take some restraint.

"Do you ever read bad reviews about your movies?" she asked, curious.

He shrugged. "Yeah, but it doesn't bother me."

"Yeah it does," she said knowingly.

"Okay, yeah it does," he laughed. "But the millions they pay me help soften the blow."

She burst out laughing, covering her mouth with her hand to avoid spitting out her pop. "I cannot believe you just went there."

He shot her a devilish grin. Then the lights dimmed and she reached over and took his hand in hers as the opening scene unfolded. Storm knew she did it as a gesture of support and he sat in wonder at how much he'd grown to depend on it.

Abby was mesmerized the entire movie. Action packed, a few corny lines, but Storm was brilliant. He dazzled on the big screen. She also loved the way he shifted in his seat as he watched himself. She could tell it made him uncomfortable. It wasn't the false modesty or feigned humility he showered on the press. His discomfort was genuine. To Abby, it was both adorable and refreshing to witness small insecurities in a man that seemed untouchable and larger than life.

When the ending credits rolled, there was a buzz of excitement.

"They loved it," she whispered to Storm, giving his hand a reassuring squeeze.

He shrugged with indifference, but she could tell he was relieved.

A press booth was set up outside the theater. The partially blocked off street was thick with cameras and reporters. Storm took a seat at the booth. His sister managed to avoid the spotlight and slipped away after the show, but Harry sat on one side of Storm and Abby on the other. Dressed in a white t-shirt, dark jeans, and a black ball cap, Abby couldn't recall when Storm had looked sexier. Or more at ease.

Most of the questions from the press were softballs and Storm fielded them easily. But whenever a reporter threw him a curveball, he remained poised and charming.

"Wasn't this movie just a replica of the last one, with no new substance?" one reporter asked.

"Well, c'mon now Larry, I was seated only two rows behind you and you seemed pretty into the movie." He tilted his head to the side and grinned. "In fact, if I'm not mistaken, I think you even cheered during that final fight scene."

Larry's face went red and the rest of the press erupted with laughter.

"Okay folks, that's all we have time for today," Harry cut in after thirty minutes of questions. Abby stood to her feet, relieved it was over. She felt like a mannequin, smile plastered on her face through the entire ordeal. As she stood to leave, she heard a female member of the press shout out a question aimed at her.

"Abigail, how does it feel to be Storm's 'It' girl of the week?"

The question was condescending and mean. Taking a page out of Storm's book, she took it in stride. "Well," she said, "as disappointing as this news might be, I plan to stick around for far longer than a week." With smug satisfaction, she rounded the booth to head for the limo. She was done with the limelight.

As she stepped away from the table that formed a protective barrier between her and the press, the throng of reporters pressed in closer. Cameras flashed. Questions flew. In a panic, Abby glanced around for Storm and the bodyguard, but she was surrounded before either could get to her.

Microphones and cameras were thrust in her face. When she tried to press through the madness, she was struck by something. She couldn't be sure if it was a camera or the shoulder of an overzealous reporter, but the unexpected blow knocked her to the ground.

Through the chaos, she heard the enraged growl from Storm—a sound half human, half wounded animal. He leapt over the booth and shoved reporters aside to get to her. The bodyguard trailed close behind.

Abby tried to protest that she was okay, but Storm scooped her into his arms, then plunked her into the outstretched arms of his bodyguard.

"Drive her back to my room," he barked. His boyish charm was temporarily replaced with dark-seeded anger. Once Abby was safely out of harm's way, he turned and glared into the faces of the press. Normally he was good with the media. Never standoffish or snide. But this time they'd gone too far.

"She didn't sign up for this," he shouted into the abyss of flashing cameras.

His manager stepped in beside him and placed a firm hand on his shoulder. "Storm, you need to calm down."

"I won't calm down," he seethed. His eyes never wavered from the crowd. "She's not a public figure. You hear me? You need to back off." Then he turned and stalked away, leaving Harry behind to do damage control.

Harry held up his hands. "Ladies and gentlemen of the press. Understandably, my client is a little upset right now…"

Storm shook his head in anger as he stalked past the barricade signs and hailed a cab. *Upset* didn't begin to cover how he was feeling.

Pausing outside Abby's open door of the hotel suite, Storm knocked twice on the doorframe. "May I come in?" he asked, poking his head inside.

She was sitting up in bed. "Of course." She smiled up at him but he remained in the doorway. "Storm, yes, please come in," she said louder, assuming he hadn't heard her.

He had indeed heard her but he was shocked how calm she seemed sitting up in bed and flipping through the television channels as if it was any ordinary evening. He also worried that once he came in and they had a chance to talk, she'd reveal recent events were too much for her and that she wished to end the assignment. Storm didn't want things to end yet. He'd grown used to having her around.

He walked slowly toward the bed, then sat down beside her. "I'm sorry about all that," he said after a bit.

"Storm, I'm fine. It wasn't a big deal. Manic reporters and aggressive cameramen are part of the business. They just add to the excitement," she teased. If she was being honest, the events of the past few days had shaken her up a bit, but she was tough. It would take more than a couple bumps and bruises to scare her away.

Reaching over to stroke her cheek, Storm felt at a loss for words. His brow furrowed.

"Stop worrying about me. Honestly, you're worse than my mother."

He laughed but the worried expression didn't leave his face. "Speaking of your mother," he said. "She called me when I was in the elevator to ask what happened and make sure you were alright. I guess the story already broke."

"Really? How did she get your number?"

"Apparently she called Tammie, who gave her Patty's number; and then Patty caved under the pressure." He shook his head, doing his best to shake away the thought of losing her.

Abby misinterpreted the gesture as his disapproval. Reaching for his hand, she said, "Well, I hope you don't fault Patty. My mother can be very persua…"

She didn't have time to finish her sentence. Storm pulled her into his arms and held her close. "Abby, the bodyguard stays," he demanded as he buried his face in her hair.

She didn't argue. Instead, she leaned into him and took comfort that, in that moment, he needed her as much as she needed him.

CHAPTER FIFTEEN

"*We* made page six," Storm yelled from the living area of their suite. "Want to celebrate with dinner tonight?"

"I'm afraid I have a thing tonight," Abby admitted shyly as she entered the room, not bothering to look at the article.

"What sort of a thing?" he asked, setting down the newspaper and patting the seat beside him on the couch.

"Well, it turns out my boss is so happy with your new, shiny image, she's throwing me a party and giving me a raise."

"Abby that's awesome." He planted a kiss on her cheek.

"Well, I'm not sure about the raise, but the party part is true. You don't mind, do you? I feel sort of bad, actually." She shot him an apologetic look. With so many people clambering to get a piece of him, she didn't want to be perceived as one of them.

"Hey, you've worked hard. Who knew you could tame the storm?" he quipped, referring to the many articles they'd both enjoyed over the past two weeks.

Abby laughed, still nervous and feeling a bit tongue-tied. She wanted to invite him to go with her but was worried he'd turn her down.

"What time?" he asked.

"Seven," she said, perking up once she thought he might be interested.

"Okay, I can probably keep myself busy for a few hours."

Her shoulders drooped. "Oh, okay. I mean, you can always come," she offered.

"That's okay, Cricket, I wouldn't want to intrude. Besides, that might be awkward for Tammie. I know she never liked me."

"I'm sure she likes you fine," she lied, trying her best to mask her disappointment and the coolness she felt every time he called her that nickname. She smiled up at him, pushing the hurt aside. She wanted to make the most out of the time she had left with him. Once the movie was released, who knew… "Well, you have me until then," she said more cheerily than she felt. "What would you like to do?"

Storm's eyes flickered to the bedroom and Abby laughed, despite her growing sorrow.

In a room full of people, Abby wondered how it was possible to feel so utterly alone and wished for the thousandth time Storm was with her so he could celebrate with her. She stepped outside for some air, hoping to dodge the emptiness closing in around her. She'd felt deflated when he didn't offer to go with her. *Hadn't she rearranged her whole life to attend everything he'd wanted?* Then again, she was being paid to do so. Perhaps that was a sticking point with him.

When she strolled over to the wooden bench located outside the exit door, she was surprised to discover she wasn't the only one sneaking out of the party.

An attractive young woman in a blue cocktail dress was sitting on the bench, puffing on a cigarette. Abby paused to watch as the woman closed her eyes, slowly inhaling the nicotine, and then carefully blowing the smoke out and away from her. This ritual seemed to bring the woman comfort somehow, and for the first time Abby found herself wishing she too was a smoker.

As if reading Abby's thoughts, the young woman stretched her slender hand towards her, offering her cigarette case. "Would you like one?"

Realizing she had been staring longingly at the woman's cigarette, Abby grew self-conscious. "Err…no thanks. I don't smoke." Now she worried that she sounded like she was judging.

"Suit yourself," the woman replied, turning her attention away from Abby and back to the cigarette. But the woman scooted over to make room for her on the bench so Abby figured she must not have been too offended at her refusal of the offering. She took a seat beside the lady, stretched out her legs, and kicked off her shoes. Fighting the urge to rub her feet, she made a silent vow to never again wear such high heels.

"I hate these parties," the woman admitted, echoing Abby's unspoken sentiments. "I can't believe I have to waste a perfectly good night to celebrate some self-important big-wig at my husband's work when he and I should be out celebrating something about our own lives." The woman stuck out a pouty lip and took another drag of her cigarette. "So, who are you with?" she finally asked.

Abby could feel her cheeks redden. "I'm here by myself."

"Oh, so you must work at Caldwell's." As mortified as Abby was that this inquiry was continuing, she started to find the humor in it.

"Yep. I *am* the self-important big-wig," Abby told her bluntly, but she smiled and extended her hand to the woman. "I'm Abigail Travis."

"And *I'm* a complete imbecile," the woman said, returning the handshake and flushing crimson.

Abby laughed. "No worries, I totally get it. Believe me, I wouldn't be here if this little party wasn't, you know, for me. My boss likes to overdo things sometimes," she explained, feeling both apologetic and amused.

The woman apologized again, stamped out her cigarette, then made an excuse to rejoin the party. Abby reasoned the woman probably wanted to put as much distance between their awkward conversation as she could, and she really couldn't blame her.

Alone once more with her thoughts and aching feet, she reached down to rub the ball of her foot, still laughing at the woman's obvious discomfort.

"Is this seat taken," she heard a familiar voice say. When she looked up, she was stunned to find Storm standing before her, all dolled up in a tux.

"You came!" She sprung from the bench and wrapped her arms around his neck.

"I couldn't stay away," he admitted. "I'm sorry, Abby, I wanted to make sure the spotlight was on you tonight, and I worried my being here might ruin that. But selfishly, I missed you."

"You're a silly, thoughtful man," she laughed. Her eyes glistened with happiness. "I'm happy to share a spotlight with you anytime. Besides, what's one last pull for publicity before your film comes out?" She slipped back into her shoes and pulled him towards the party. "Let's dance," she said. "Tonight, we'll get your fans all riled up."

CHAPTER SIXTEEN

*A*bby found herself dreading her last day at the Wylderton. Tomorrow Storm's movie would be officially released. He was more popular than ever. The studio was pleased with his new image and Storm and Harry were actively negotiating a new contract. While she was happy for him, the thought of losing him for good was weighing heavy on her mind. And heart.

She had only herself to blame, she realized. Her attempts at keeping things professional had failed. She loved him. Loved him deeply. She knew he had feelings for her too. She wasn't blind. But they were from two different worlds. Once her assignment ended, she knew Storm would move on. She didn't blame him. It was just the way things were. He had his world and she had hers.

"Tomorrow's the big day," Storm announced cheerily.

He marveled at everything they'd been through. Aggressive press. Stinging insults. An overzealous fan who'd bribed a maid for a keycard and had been caught naked in his hotel suite. Storm had been angry. Abby had just laughed and asked, *"Oh, c'mon, can you really blame her?"* Her ability to take things in stride always caught him by surprise.

Harry had helped him work out the final arrangements on his contract. He was looking forward to sharing the news with her, and for whatever might come next.

Abby fought to hide the gut punch Storm's cheery words brought. Despite how close they'd become, he hadn't mentioned one word about what life might hold for them once tomorrow arrived. Forcing a smile, she said, "I'm so happy for you."

Storm was puzzled by her melancholy expression but he didn't press her on it.

Her mother called to invite her to dinner. "You okay?" she asked when she heard the distress in Abby's voice that she was trying so hard to mask.

"Of course. Why do you ask?"

"I can tell when my baby is sad."

Abby wanted to share her heartbreak with her mother but speaking it aloud would make it all the more real. "Mom, I'm completely fine, really."

"Did he break your heart?" she asked. "Because if he did, I'm going to go there and give that man a piece of my mind. He doesn't deserve you."

A tear slipped down her cheek but she kept her tone chipper. "Mom, he didn't break my heart. We were just together for fun and now it's coming to an end. Honestly, I feel nothing for him. I mean, he's an *actor*."

When Abby hung up the phone, she knew she'd convinced her mother but she hadn't managed to convince herself. She wandered out of her room feeling miserable.

"So that's really how you feel?" Storm asked when she entered their shared living area.

Fear gripped her heart when she realized he'd likely heard every word. "What?" she asked, feigning ignorance.

"It was all an act? None of it was real?" His voice shook with anger. But beyond that, the sadness in his eyes revealed she had wounded him.

His hurt was an act, Abby told herself, but she couldn't bring herself to respond.

"Answer me. You owe me that much. Your feelings for me— they're not real, is that what you're claiming?" His eyes raged like the sea.

Protect your heart, the voice in Abby's head shouted above the dread settling in her stomach. "Yes," she said flatly. "I was just caught up in the fairytale and all the press. We both were."

"It was more than that and you know it."

"Was it?" she challenged.

He narrowed his eyes, fixing his gaze on her. "It was for me."

"You're an actor. How am I supposed to believe anything you say?" She regretted the words the moment they slipped past her lips. She wished she could rein them back in, but it was too late. They hung in the air like a thick fog. She found it hard to breathe. Were there no limits to how far she would go to protect her heart—even at the expense of the man she loved?

"Storm, I..."

"Forget it," he said. "I get it. I'm just an actor. No worries. We actors are pretty shallow people. I'll get over it quickly." He shrugged and headed towards the door, but Abby could sense his deep sorrow and observed the stoop of his shoulders, a contradiction to his typically ram rod posture.

Nondisclosure agreement be damned, the first thing she could think to do was call her mother back. She was sobbing by the time her mom picked up the phone. "Honey? Honey what's wrong, I can't understand you."

"He left. He left," is all she could manage.

She realized her mistake once her mother began with her, *I told you so's*, followed by her account of the kind of man she *knew* Storm was. It infuriated her. "No, Mom. It was me. I drove him away. He was wonderful. I was just so afraid of being hurt. I've got to fix this." And without another word, she hung up the phone and raced from the hotel room in search of Storm.

"Patty, I know he probably told you not to tell anyone where he was going, but I really need to speak with him." Abby was growing more desperate with each phone call.

"Ma'am, I promise you, I haven't heard from him," his assistant said.

The cold, formal way Patty addressed her made Abby suspect the assistant might know more than she was willing to reveal.

"Okay, thank you," Abby murmured, ending the call, and continuing her pursuit of Storm, hoping she wasn't too late. Her stomach churned at the thought of him finding solace in the arms of an endearing fan or other casual acquaintance. *We actors are pretty shallow people*, his words echoed in her ears. She hoped that wasn't true.

Fueled by espresso and her feelings of stupidity, she spent hours searching every spot she could think of, including the quiet Italian restaurant they'd shared just two weeks earlier. As she pulled away from the restaurant, a young boy on a skateboard darted in front of her car. She slammed on her breaks. Coffee sloshed in the cup holder but the boy whisked down the road, unaware of his close brush with disaster.

Heart now in her throat, Abby continued her search but when her efforts proved unfruitful, she returned to their hotel suite. She was exhausted and hysterical—and more thankful than ever for the back entryway and service elevator.

She held her breath when she reached her suite, opening the door slowly in hopes of seeing Storm stretched out on the couch. Heck, she'd even settle for him being there with another woman if he'd just return to her. Well, maybe not.

But disappointment flooded her when she discovered their hotel suite was still empty. She called the front desk to check for messages. There weren't any. Abandoning all hope, she sank down on the couch, pulled her knees to her chest, and had a good cry.

When Storm returned later that evening, he spotted Abby sitting by herself on the couch, clutching a book, although she didn't appear to be reading it. She looked up when he entered the room, and the smudge of mascara in the corners of her eyes revealed she may have been crying. Perhaps something in the book had moved her to tears. Or maybe she'd gone for a jog and the smudges were caused by perspiration. But as Storm approached her, he felt confident she had been crying. Tiny tearstains streaked her soft, flushed cheeks.

"I'm sorry," he started. "If you're worried about your job…"

Abby leapt from the couch and into his arms. The look of surprise on his face would have been comical if she wasn't so desperate to patch things up.

"Hey, hey, what's wrong?" he asked when she began to cry again. Deep sobs racked her body.

"Storm… Jack. I'm so sorry. I know there was more to what happened between us than I was willing to admit. It was cruel of me to say what I said. I didn't mean any of it."

"Hey, it's fine." He shrugged.

"It's not fine, and you know it." Growing impatient, she stepped back to look at him, recognizing his devil-may-care defense mechanism.

"Okay, it's not fine," he said, his anger resurfacing. "I get that I have a reputation. I get that you're scared. But I'm scared too. This is all new to me. Very new to me. I gave you every opportunity to walk away. No regrets, remember?"

"I remember," she said indignantly.

"Okay then. Let's give us a chance to work. I don't want to sabotage what we have before we get a chance to figure out what *this* is." He pointed to her, to himself, then back to her.

"Storm, I'd be miserable in the spotlight all the time. I need simplicity."

"I know," he told her. "Abby, after my next movie, I'm out."

"What? No, I can't let you do that."

"It's not for you. Well, maybe that was the tipping point," he admitted. "But I did this for me. I've agreed to do the final movie on my contract, then I'm done. I didn't extend my contract."

"Storm…"

"I want to do something different. That's what Harry has been helping me with, actually. I plan to simplify things. My place is going up for sale. I've invested in a winery with a vineyard I'm going to help run. Instead of studying scripts, I'll be learning all about soil preparation, pruning, and wine crates."

Abby was stunned. "Wow, I had no idea."

"Abby, I want this for us. I can't lose you. I want us to work."

Her tone cooled and she crossed her arms in front of her chest. "Well walking out was a funny way of showing you wanted to work things out."

"I needed time to think."

"Good for you," she sniffed. "While you were out *thinking* did it occur to you that I might be here, crying myself into a frenzy while drinking day-old wine straight out of the bottle and sobbing my way through every word of Purple Rain?"

He shot her a sideways look. "What?"

"What? Nothing. I'm kidding." She wasn't kidding, of course. She had done all those things. "Where were you anyways?" she asked, not sure if she wanted to know the answer.

"I went to your place."

Her expression softened and her tone turned to one of disbelief. "You did?"

"Well, I knew you kept a spare key under the front doormat. A horrible hiding place by the way. And I also knew it was the last place anyone would look and I needed some time to collect my thoughts. Besides, your place makes me feel ... at home."

Abby smiled. She wrapped her arms around his neck and planted a kiss on his neck. Being with him made her feel at home. "So, with your place going up for sale...?"

"I was hoping you were searching for a roommate," he said with a nervous grin.

"Well, I'm still not quite convinced you'd make a very good roommate." But she was already settling into the idea as she pressed her lips against his.

"Wait, where did you think I went?" he finally asked, pulling back from their embrace.

She shifted uncomfortably from foot to foot, biting her lip and peering up at him sheepishly.

"You really don't think much of me still, do you?" But he was smiling. "I can work to change all that." He pulled her closer.

"You don't have to work on anything. I was too worried about keeping my own emotions under wraps to see the real you. That's on me."

"I'd say you make me want to be a better man, but I fear that might sound like a line."

Abby laughed. "Well I'm sure old habits die hard."

"Damn, I love you," he told her for the first time as he stroked her hair.

"Another line?" she teased, but tears of joy welled up in her green eyes.

"Abby, I love you," he said again, waiting patiently for an answer.

Eyes misting, she smiled up at him. "Heck, I've loved you since the night you fed me ravioli and got me drunk on the wine flight."

He looked relieved. "Maybe you just fell in love with the ravioli."

"Well, I think that's still the start of something meaningful." Then her tone changed from playful to sincere. "But seriously, you know I love you, right?"

"I do now." He bent down to kiss her, then changed his mind. Pulling back to study her, he said, "I'm never going to take you for granted, Abby. Not ever."

"Better not, it would be terrible publicity." She laughed nervously at her own remark, then leaned in closer. "I just have one request." She raised an eyebrow and tilted her head. "A demand, really."

"Okay. Let's hear it." He looked anxious as he awaited her ultimatum. Whatever it was, he prayed he could deliver.

"No more *Cricket*. I loathe being compared to an antenna-baring bug."

"Deal," he said, relaxing his shoulders as he tried to hide his relief. "But you have to always call me Jack, then."

"Really?" It would take some getting used to, but she would do it if it meant that much to him. "Okay if that's what you want."

He paused, considering. "Nah, Storm sounds way sexier."

"I'll admit, it has grown on me," she agreed.

"You've grown on me," he said, cradling her face in his hands. She giggled as he swept her into his arms and kissed her. She didn't hold back when she kissed him in return. She no longer worried what she felt was no more than a Hollywood love story. But if that's all it was, she'd settle for the fairytale kind. Those always had a happy ending.

Marigold Summer

CHAPTER ONE

*A*ngus Barnes laid awake while his wife, Pearl, hummed in her sleep beside him. She did that sometimes. There was a time when he'd found it endearing. Now he had to fight the urge not to smother her with one of her embroidered throw pillows while she slept. He sat up in bed instead, swinging his tired legs over the side and feeling around for the comfort of his sheepskin lined slippers with his wrinkled toes. He sighed when he realized Pearl must have moved them to the closet once again. What was the point of having slippers if he had to walk across the cold floor to retrieve them? She knew it bugged him when she moved them. Just as he knew it bugged her to keep them by the bedside. "It's untidy," she'd complain.

Feeling the chill of the farm-wood floorboards beneath his bare feet, he crept out of the room, wondering all the while when the spark in his marriage had died. Perhaps faint embers still burned, just below the ash; and with a little coaxing, could be revived. But he was bone tired and lacked the energy. He realized his lack of motivation might be the answer to his question: his love had grown as cold as the floors he was now forced to walk barefoot across.

In the kitchen he poured tap water into a teakettle and set it on the stove. He lit the pilot light, turned on the burner, and rummaged through the cupboard for the tea bags, wondering where Pearl had stashed them. She was constantly arranging and rearranging things. It gave her something to do. It drove him crazy. When the kettle whistled, announcing the water had reached optimal temperature, he let the shrill sound continue for a few moments before padding over to the stove and moving the kettle to the back burner. He hoped the noise would be enough to disrupt his wife's peaceful dreams without fully rousing her.

The herbal tea was as bitter as his thoughts and he doubted it would help him get back to sleep. In a couple hours, the newspaper boy would drop off the paper, then he'd have something to do. In the meantime, he thought about Pearl and their life together. She'd made him happy once upon a time. Not over-the-moon happy like he'd been with his first wife—but probably happier than he deserved if he was honest. But lately he'd grown to resent her. Being stuck in the same room with her was like enduring nails on a blackboard. He reckoned she felt the same. He knew he'd ceased to be pleasant to live with.

For years she'd been the answer to his prayers—someone to get him through the loneliness after his first wife, Marigold, left him so abruptly. But now their thirty-year anniversary was coming up, and instead of preparing to celebrate, he was starting to believe he should prepare for a divorce. Or at least a trial separation.

By the time Pearl awoke, the morning sun was pouring through the windows and Angus had already read the paper and finished his breakfast of oatmeal and toast.

She stumbled into the brightly lit kitchen, bleary-eyed; her long, silvery brown hair in disarray. She'd stopped dyeing it a few years back. With her small frame, full lips, and heart shaped face, she was still attractive. But the deep frown lines and creases surrounding her sad, gray-green eyes revealed her age.

"I kept the leftover oatmeal on low in case you wanted any," Angus told her, realizing his thoughts had drifted and he'd probably been staring.

She offered a tight smile and asked, "Any plans for the day?" She hoped he had some. Since his retirement, Angus spent most of his time at home, shuffling around in his ratty slippers and muttering about one perceived injustice or another. Pearl was looking forward to a day without him so she could enjoy her flowerbeds and bird feeders. Maybe a hot bath in the clawfoot tub. Ages ago she'd convinced Angus to drag the corroded old tub in from the barn and restore it. There was a time when her husband was all too happy to do projects for her. Now asking him to pick up his dirty socks from the floor was more exertion than he was willing to oblige her.

"Arty and I are going fishing," Angus replied, his nose buried in the paper he'd already read.

"Oh good." Pearl's cheerful tone didn't mask her relief. "That'll be fun for you guys," she amended. He grunted in response.

Angus showered, dressed, then kissed his wife on the cheek before leaving.

"Love you," she murmured without feeling.

"Love you, too," he mumbled back, already halfway out the door. Both knew their words held no truth—but both lacked the energy to do anything about it.

CHAPTER TWO

"*E*ver tried those dating sites," Angus asked, breaking the silence. The two friends hadn't caught a bite all day, but neither minded. They had a cooler of beer, a warm breeze, and an empty riverbank. Not to mention quiet companionship.

Arty smirked, but kept his eyes focused on the glistening water. "Are you kidding me? We're too old for that. Besides, what would Pearl say?"

"It's actually for her that I'm asking."

"Say what now?" Arty sat up straight, his eyes focusing on Angus and no longer trained on the water or his fishing pole.

"We're both miserable," Angus confessed. "I don't want to be the bad guy and I think she's just looking for a reason to leave. I thought maybe if she met someone else..."

His old friend slapped him playfully on the back. "News flash. We're all miserable, buddy," he chuckled. "And I've heard of guys killing off their wives. But trying to find someone else to date them?" He hooted with laughter, took another swig of his beer, then shook his head, grinning from ear to ear. "If that doesn't just take the cake."

Angus gave his fishing pole a frustrated tug as he frowned out at the water. "Forget it," he grumbled. "It was a stupid idea." But he made a mental note to ask the neighbor kid instead. Kids were good at technology, weren't they? Perhaps his neighbor could set up a profile for Pearl.

It was dusk when Angus returned home. Pearl was at the stove, cooking dinner. She wore a navy blue and white checkered dress, the one she typically saved for town. She'd curled her hair and it hung loosely down her back. The spaghetti sauce bubbled in the pot while she hummed along to a song playing on the old kitchen radio. Her hair teased the strings of her apron as she swayed back and forth to the music.

Angus stood in the doorway of the kitchen, watching her, realizing she hadn't heard him come in. Head held high, shoulders back, and hips swaying, Pearl looked happy and at ease. Not at all the way she acted when they were together. He was full of regret at the realization. The strain on their marriage was more his fault than hers, he admitted to himself. He'd never really gotten over Marigold, a fact he was certain Pearl was aware of and had been living with all these years. On the day they'd learned he couldn't have children, the news only brought Pearl further heartache.

He walked up behind her and placed a firm hand on her shoulder. Startled, she whirled around, wooden spoon in hand, and splattered spaghetti sauce across his shirt. They both burst out laughing—sharing a rare, carefree moment. Angus pulled her into his arms and kissed her. She stood on her tiptoes, closing her eyes and parting her lips to meet his.

For a promising moment, the sparks returned. Angus caressed her cheeks with his callused hands as he lengthened the kiss. Pearl moaned softly, desperate for her husband's affections. But when the image of Marigold popped into his head, Angus stiffened. Pearl felt his reaction. Recognized it all too well. Saddened, she pulled away from his embrace, turned back to the stove, and went back to stirring the sauce. A woeful tear slipped down her cheek.

"I'm just going to wash up," Angus spoke up lamely behind her.

Shoulders slumped, Pearl nodded but didn't turn around. She couldn't bear for him to see the hurt in her eyes.

CHAPTER THREE

*A*ngus looked forward to the long drive to *Senior's Haven*, the assisted living center a few towns over from his. He loved the historical farmhouses and grand red barns that lined the roadside. He took pleasure in the way the sun danced across the rolling wheat fields; admired the acres of lush pastureland speckled with cows and sheep. It reminded him of his younger days when his farm was flourishing. He'd since sold off most of the property, having grown too old to maintain it all himself. It gave him a thrill to see other farms still thriving. But best of all, the trip gave him a chance to be alone with his thoughts.

As always, the pleasant, young assistant at the front desk greeted him with a warm smile when he signed in. He appreciated that her smile seemed genuine as opposed to one of sympathy. "Any other visitors?" he asked. She shook her head, *no*. This time her eyes held a glint of the sympathy he abhorred but he didn't fault her for it.

He walked past the front desk and made his way down the long hallway. Fluorescent light bulbs hummed and flickered as staff in scrubs bustled about. Although the center was kept immaculately clean, he always caught the faint odor of urine amongst the scent of disinfectants. When he reached his intended door and stepped into the room, it smelled of soap and bleach but he caught a whiff of the sweet perfume his mother loved to wear. He figured the nurses must have put it on her and it brought him comfort she was being so well cared for.

His mother sat in the corner of the room in her wheelchair, facing the T.V. with a quilted blanket draped over her shriveled legs.

Angus crossed the room towards her. "Hey, Momma," he said, bending down and planting a soft kiss on her creased cheek.

She didn't look up. Her eyes didn't waver from the television screen, even though he knew her vision was too far gone to see the classic western she was pretending to watch.

"They still treating you okay here?" he asked.

Still nothing.

His Momma used to have good days and bad days. Over the past few months it seemed she only had bad days and worse days. Alzheimer's—a term he'd learned to hate and had also learned could be hereditary. He doubted she even recognized him and wondered why he still made the hour drive to visit every Friday. Perhaps it was more for his benefit than hers. She was the only family he had, and he ached with loneliness at the sad reality.

"I didn't know you liked westerns," he prattled on. "Maybe next time I visit I'll bring one of my favorites. You have a VCR or DVD player in here?" He thought he saw her head move ever so slightly and chose to take it as a response to his question. He couldn't bear to think the only person on earth who genuinely loved him no longer recognized him. He thought again of Pearl; wondered if she was anxiously waiting for him back at home. Perhaps he could make an effort and take her out on a date the way he used to. As he took a seat beside his mother, he made a promise to himself to do just that.

Pearl was waiting for him when he arrived home but it wasn't with open arms. Instead, there was a suitcase beside her on the floor and she was tapping her foot impatiently.

"Where have you been?" Her eyes were dark with anger; accusatory.

"Visiting Momma." He kept his tone light and cheery, remembering his promise and hoping to avoid another exhausting argument.

"Oh," she said, softening a little. "Well, I've been waiting around to tell you I'm leaving."

For a moment he felt a ray of hope she was leaving him for good, but then he realized a single suitcase wouldn't be enough to hold her belongings. "Where you going?"

"My sister needs some help around her place. The farm is going to poo since Charles died and those worthless kids of hers aren't pitching in, so now I'm going to have to drive there myself and help her out."

Pearl never could bring herself to curse. Everything was *poo* and *tarnation*; *fiddle sticks* when she was real upset. It was another one of those things Angus had found charming when they first met but had grown to loathe in recent years. He opened his mouth to tell his wife it wasn't her job to take care of her sister, but realizing it might make her stay, he thought better of it. "Give her my best," he said instead.

Pearl shot him a sideways look. It was clear she'd expected a different reaction. Perhaps she'd wanted him to talk her out of it and beg her to stay. She placed her hands on her hips, pursed her lips, and let out a loud, exasperated sigh. When this still didn't garner a reaction from her husband of almost thirty years, she picked up her suitcase and marched out the front door.

CHAPTER FOUR

*W*ith Pearl out of town, Angus took advantage of his newfound freedom. He made lots of time to go fishing with Arty. It gave him immense satisfaction to scale and clean the fish he brought home after spending the day at the riverbank. Some days he spent hours tinkering with the old farm truck behind the shed. He never got it started, but that was never really the point. He even camped under the stars in his backyard a night or two. The next day his old bones would groan in protest, but it was worth the feel of the crisp morning air on his face.

He wasn't sure why he didn't do more of what he loved while his wife was home. She would probably enjoy having her own time away from him. Perhaps he'd thought spending more time with her would alleviate the guilt he carried for harboring feelings for his first wife. It didn't, of course, and not allowing Pearl her space likely drove a deeper wedge between them.

"How's Pearl," Arty asked as they sat on the riverbank gulping down the turkey sandwiches Arty's wife had prepared. It was the first real meal Angus had had in a week.

"She's good," Angus said with a shrug as he took a swig of beer to wash down his sandwich. The sun was beating down on his back, he'd consumed more beers then he'd planned to, and he was feeling a bit lightheaded. "I think she's enjoying our time apart." He didn't sound bitter. Only matter of fact.

"That's good. That's good." Arty wanted to tease him about the dating site but thought better of it. "What about you? How have you been?" he asked instead.

Angus grunted. "Momma's been slipping more." It pained him to admit it aloud. He dreaded the day when his momma would no longer be around.

His old friend nodded, then slapped at a mosquito. The fish weren't biting that day, but the mosquitos weren't having any trouble. They raged relentless amongst the tall reeds of the riverbank.

Angus continued. "It gets lonely in that old house, but it's not Pearl I miss." The combination of heat and alcohol were causing him to reveal more than he'd intended.

Arty nodded again and cleared his throat, uncomfortable. It was the most his friend had ever opened up to him. "Life can get tough sometimes." He raised his beer in one hand, slapped Angus on the back with the other, and flashed him a goofy grin. "That's why they invented beer and fishing."

"Yep," Angus said, laughing despite himself. "Thank the good Lord for beer and fishing." He felt a nibble on his line but didn't react. He was enjoying his inebriated, semi-dehydrated stupor. He closed his eyes, threw back his head, and invited the sunrays to continue their assault on his balding head.

CHAPTER FIVE

When he entered his mother's room at the assisted living center, Angus noticed she appeared more alert than usual. Someone had braided her silvery-red hair and changed her into a cheery, floral dress. She looked up from the television and flashed him a grin.

"Angus, my boy, how have you been?"

Angus practically tripped over himself to reach her. He took her by the hand and gave it a tight squeeze. "How are you Momma?"

"You haven't visited me in a while," she scolded.

"Momma, I come every Friday."

"Hmph." She crossed her arms in front of her chest. "Just because you moved out to be on your own doesn't mean you can't come visit your Momma's house."

His stomach jolted when he realized she wasn't as coherent as he'd originally thought. He wondered how old she thought he was. Even still, it was nice she remembered who he was.

"I'll try to do better, Momma." He continued to hold her frail hand in his, stroking it gently with his thumb.

His mother narrowed her eyes at him. "Is that new wife of yours keeping you away?" she asked in a teasing voice.

Angus felt his mood sour at the mere mention of his wife; but he also felt the need to defend her. "Don't blame Pearl, Momma."

"Pearl? Are you young kids giving each other silly nicknames now? I'm talking about Marigold."

The sound of Marigold's name rolling so casually off his mother's tongue felt like a swift punch to the gut. Angus swallowed hard, doing his best to ignore the pain and sorrow that bubbled up inside him.

When Angus had first met Marigold at the local feed and supply store, he'd known straight away he loved her. They'd haggled over the last bag of chicken feed, but one sharp look from her cornflower blue eyes and Angus had relented, handing over the feed bag and his heart in one fail swoop. He'd shown up on her doorstep later that evening, expecting to charm her with a bushel of marigolds. Instead, the flowers had thrown her into a sneezing fit. Turned out she was highly allergic to the very flower she'd been named after. But the gesture had won her heart just the same and the two were married later that same year. They'd been happy, for a time. Even blissfully so. Then one day, without warning, she'd left him.

Swallowing the lump in his throat, Angus looked his mother in the eye, prepared to tell her the tragic truth. The love of his life, Marigold, was gone and there was only Pearl. Pearl who had been a faithful, devoted wife for almost thirty years; but somehow was not enough to fill the void Marigold had left behind. As Angus held his mother's gaze, seeking the right words, he noticed her eyes were clearer than they had been in some time. He cleared his throat, then whispered, "Marigold sends her love."

It wasn't very often he spoke his first wife's name but he got a pleasureful thrill when he did. He felt his mood lifting and the storm clouds that raged in his soul parted to make way for the sun.

"She's going to bake you a pie for next week, you know," Angus continued with the charade. Despite the initial shock of hearing her name, it was oddly comforting to be able to discuss Marigold as if she were waiting for him back at home. While they were married, she'd always greeted him at the door with open arms, no matter the weather.

"Blueberry, I hope."

"Huh?" He'd been lost in thought.

"I hope it's a blueberry pie," his mother spoke louder, assuming her volume of speech was the problem.

"Of course. She knows it's your favorite." He licked his lips, recalling that Marigold used to make the most delicious blueberry pies.

He stayed longer than he'd intended. Being able to talk to someone else about Marigold, someone who'd also known and loved her, was a comfort. And it felt good to have his mother remember his name, even if her recollections were a few decades off.

A nurse knocked on the door. "Visiting hours are over, I'm afraid." Her kind eyes held an apology.

Momma nodded. Her eyes were starting to cloud and Angus recognized she was slipping back into herself. He bent down and kissed her cheek.

She patted his hand and whispered, "Give my best to Marigold."

As he left the room, heart full, Angus had to admit, today was one of Momma's good days.

Angus thought of Marigold on the drive home, realizing he couldn't remember why she'd left. They had once been so happy. The envy of all their friends. He searched his memories but couldn't recall them growing apart; couldn't even recollect them having a fight. He twisted his wedding ring around his finger as he drove. When he did, the image of Pearl popped into his head and he stopped fiddling with the ring and returned his thoughts to Marigold. Her presence filled the truck cab, casting a pall of bittersweet memories.

He parked at the end of the drive. He needed a walk to clear his head. As he walked the long, gravel driveway, Angus kept his head down. The gravel crunched noisily beneath his feet as he shuffled along at a snail's pace. He dreaded going back to that empty house so filled with memories. Bittersweet reminiscences of Marigold and the times they'd spent there. Years of memories with Pearl who had once made him happy but now the thought of her filled him with apprehension.

He stopped in his tracks when something small but bright caught his eye. Ahead of him was a single marigold, springing up beside the pathway. Its bold, orange color was like a burst of sunshine amongst the ash-colored gravel.

Increasing his pace, he walked over to examine it. He thought about picking it, then reconsidered. It was important that the flower live—that it grow and thrive. Knees creaking in protest, he bent down to feel the soft petals between his fingertips, careful not to crush the pungent petals with his clumsy hands. Angus sat down on the roadside, closed his eyes, and pleaded for Marigold to return to him. His tired eyes gave into his exhaustion and grief, and he let the tears flow down the creases of his face.

CHAPTER SIX

*A*fter another sun-soaked day of fishing and drinking, Arty drove Angus home, though neither were fit to drive. Their sweat drenched shirts stuck to the bench seat as they rode along in silence.

"You going to be okay?" Arty asked, putting the truck in park at the end of the drive and turning to face his friend. Angus had been melancholy all day. At first Arty had tried to carry the conversation but had given up after a time.

Grumbling something incomprehensible, Angus nodded and climbed out of the truck. After grabbing his pole and half-empty bucket of fish from the truck bed, he waved goodbye to his old friend before turning and stumbling down the long driveway.

Marigold was waiting for him when he reached his front porch. Sobered, the bucket and rod fell from his hand. The fish water slopped over his shoes but he didn't notice or care. He remained frozen on the bottom porch step, studying her in awe. She was such a beautiful sight. Despite the decades that had passed, she looked the same as the day she'd left him. Her eyes were as blue as the cornflowers that lined the highway heading into town. She'd kept her golden hair a medium length, long enough to pull back into a ponytail whenever she wished. She had never been one of those skinny girls. His own mother had once described her as plump. But to Angus, she was perfect. Soft and curvy. She had a giggle that forced everyone else to join in her laughter.

While they were together, whenever she was disheartened, which wasn't often, he'd bring her silk flowers and travel magazines and tell her about the adventures they'd go on once they'd saved enough money. Before long, her sadness would lift and she'd start talking animatedly about the places she'd loved to visit.

"You came back," Angus whispered in disbelief.

Marigold nodded. "I'm sorry I stayed away so long. But I'm here now."

No further words of apology or forgiveness were spoken between them. They sat down on the front porch swing. Angus recalled Marigold used to love to snuggle on the swing and listen to the sound of the rain dancing on the metal gable roof. She'd gaze across the cornfields and dream aloud about the places she'd like to go and about the sort of parents they'd be. They never got the chance to do either together—travel or be parents.

But today Angus wasn't weighed down with regret and sadness. He reached out and took Marigold's hand in is. Her hand was soft and inviting; just as he remembered it. The pair gazed up at the heavens, enjoying the sunlight on their faces. The wind tickled their cheeks and ruffled their hair. But it was a warm wind. The perfect weather for a perfect afternoon.

Pearl called later to tell Angus she'd be staying longer with her sister. Her sister's farm was in worse disrepair than she'd first realized. The couple tried to make casual conversation about what they'd been up to but Pearl seemed tired and Angus was aloof; his mind was elsewhere.

"Well, then, I'll call you when I can," Pearl said, keeping her voice pleasant. If Angus had been paying attention, he'd have caught her melancholy tone. She'd hoped their time apart would make him miss her—would make her miss him. Neither seemed to be working. She didn't end the call by telling him she loved him. "Talk to you soon," she said instead.

Angus echoed her words, then hung up the phone.

Pearl waited on the line a moment longer, desperate to hold onto their final moments as a couple. When she eventually hung up the phone, and heard the definitive click, she knew it was over between them. She wasn't devastated. A little regretful as she recalled how good it had once been. But all in all, she'd known this day was coming for a while. Now she'd have to find a way to make peace with it.

CHAPTER SEVEN

*I*t had been days since Pearl had called, but Marigold came to visit Angus each day. Some mornings she was waiting for him on the front porch when he woke up. Other days she didn't show up until the early evening. Angus always prepared them a simple meal of broth and potatoes, but both barely touched the food. Angus was too excited around her to eat and he guessed his inadequate culinary skills were contributing to Marigold's lack of appetite. He reckoned she ate before she came.

She didn't attempt to explain what she'd been up to all those years—just as she didn't explain what she did during the hours she wasn't with him. Angus figured she was remarried with a family of her own, so he resisted the urge to pry about her absences.

They never went out—which made Angus happy. After years of enduring her absence, he now had his Marigold all to himself. The hours were spent playing Gin Rummy, listening to vinyl records, talking about old times, or sitting quietly on the front porch, their fingers interlaced and Marigold's head on his shoulder. When they both grew tired, Marigold would announce it was time to leave. Angus knew they both had their reasons why she couldn't stay the night. He didn't dwell on it. He knew he could face the lonely nights if it meant the new day would bring her back to him.

"I'll pick us up some travel magazines from the store tomorrow," Angus offered when Marigold was preparing to leave for the evening.

Her eyes shone with excitement. "I'd like that very much."

He watched her with wonder as she walked down the long driveway and eventually disappeared from his sight.

CHAPTER EIGHT

Crowley's Family Grocer was located thirty miles outside of town, nestled between a coffee shop and a tractor repair service station. Angus discovered it while looking for a gas station on one of his drives to visit his mother. The family-owned grocery store was small. It didn't carry his favorite brand of pipe tobacco nor did the owners accept credit cards without a sizeable fee. But its customers didn't know anything about Pearl or his past and therefore the store was perfect.

Angus made a point of dropping in often. On his first visit he introduced himself and took note of the store owner's name—Rita. She was a plump, middle-aged woman with deep lines in her face but a pretty smile. By his third visit, Rita remembered his name.

"How are you doing today, Angus?" she asked politely from behind the counter.

"Amazingly well, Rita, how are you?" he answered back.

It would take a few more visits before he told the owner about Marigold. When he did, he referred to her as his wife. He talked all about her homemade pies, her love of travel, and how she was waiting for him back at home. His visits were lengthy, and Rita often had her husband take her place behind the counter so he could mind the other customers while she tended to Angus. She sensed he needed the attention. And the companionship.

A couple weeks in, Rita began to suspect something about Marigold. "You can tell when there's a woman in a man's life," she told her husband over dinner. "His shirt would be pressed, he'd be well-fed as opposed to being reed thin, and he wouldn't be spending so much time hanging around our store." Still, she never let Angus know her suspicions. She even ordered in silk marigolds after he mentioned how much his wife loved them.

Angus received the news of his mother's death on a Thursday, one day before he was set for his weekly visit. His tone was detached when he called to break the news to Pearl. She offered to drive back for the service, but he insisted he was fine and wanted to face it alone. He remained stoic as he made the funeral arrangements and notified Momma's few remaining friends who'd outlived her.

He brought a bushel of silk yellow and orange marigolds to the funeral and sat them on the pew beside him. Marigold hadn't been able to come with him that day, but the bright flowers reminded him of her and brought him comfort. Angus knew he could face anything if he had Marigold in his corner. Even the death of his mother.

CHAPTER NINE

*A*rty called to see how Angus was fairing after his mother's passing and to invite him to go fishing. It had been weeks since they'd spent the day together. Arty worried his friend's absence meant he'd grown too depressed to go anywhere. Angus had been distant at the funeral, impassive even, but Arty knew people grieved in different ways. He'd also noted that Pearl wasn't at the service, something he found strange, but not completely surprising. Angus had barely mentioned Pearl since she'd left to see her sister a couple months back.

To Arty's surprise and relief, Angus sounded upbeat on the phone. But he declined the fishing invite, saying he had other plans, though he gave no indication of what his plans were. When Arty hung up, he wondered if his old friend had tried the dating site after all and had found success. He felt a pang of jealousy but couldn't reconcile if it was due to missing his friend or if he was envious of the idea that Angus may have found love again when Arty himself was in it for the long haul with a woman who was barely more than a stranger to him.

"That was Arty," Angus told Marigold when he placed the phone back on its cradle. "He wanted to go fishing."

She smiled back at him. "You could go, you know."

He shook his head. "I'd rather stay here with you. Besides, remember I said I'd finish building those window boxes today."

"We haven't finished installing the bookshelves in the dining room either," she reminded him.

He stroked the stubble on his chin and wondered how long it had been since he'd shaved. "You're right. I need to find the right tools. I couldn't find them in the shed. Maybe I let Arty borrow them."

"You could try looking in the attic," she offered.

Angus paused, considering. He'd always avoided the attic. Couldn't quite recall why. It was sort of drafty and the ladder was a bit rickety. He patted Marigold's hand and imagined how her blue eyes would light up once he'd installed the window boxes and placed the silk flowers inside.

"What were we talking about?" he asked after a long pause.

Marigold giggled the carefree laugh he'd always loved. "Finishing projects. Tools. The attic," she reminded him.

"Yes, yes I suppose I should go up there and look for my tools. But let's play another round of Gin Rummy instead."

As he dealt the cards, he whistled an old tune he used to sing to her on the nights she couldn't sleep.

CHAPTER TEN

*A*ngus came across the antique wooden chest while rooting around the attic for his tools. It was tucked away in the corner and half buried under a stack of quilts and discarded magazines. The lock was rusting, but the rest of the trunk remained in reasonable shape. Curious, he cleared the stack of odds and ends from the top, wiped off the layers of dust with the corner of a quilt, then pried open the lock with a crowbar that hung from a stud on the unfinished walls.

Inside the dusty trunk were Marigold's belongings. Black and white photographs, love letters he knew he'd written her, their wedding china with the soft, pink floral pattern; all the things he knew she'd once treasured. He rubbed his chin, wondering to himself why she'd left it all behind. He'd have to show everything to her when she came over for dinner. He picked up a book packed away next to a neatly folded stack of clothes and old picture frames and softly brushed aside a fine layer of dust with his fingertips. It was a worn copy of *Pride and Prejudice*, Marigold's favorite novel.

When he opened the book, a folded-up slip of paper fell out of its tattered pages. He bent down to retrieve it, his old bones protesting at his sudden movements. There were two pieces of paper, he realized. The first was a half-sheet containing a grocery list. Marigold's handwriting was unmistakable—neat, curvy cursive letters. She'd always prided herself on her penmanship. The list was folded up with a newspaper clipping. Angus retrieved his reading glasses from his shirt pocket. He held the clipping close to his face as he read the headline aloud.

LOCAL PEDESTRIAN HIT BY TRUCK; KILLED INSTANTLY.

He stumbled backwards, stunned. He didn't need to read the rest. He knew what it would say. The article slipped out of his hands as memories of that nightmarish day came flooding back to him.

He'd received the news while he was at work—had scarcely believed it. While Marigold was walking home from the store on a summer afternoon, a truck had rounded the corner too fast and struck her. It had been a bright, sunny day and they'd made plans to have a picnic that same evening. That's why she'd gone to the store. To pick up a few things for their picnic. Full of regrets, he tried to recall whose idea the picnic had been. Perhaps if he'd suggested taking her out to dinner and a movie instead—though he knew they would have been too poor for that. Just as they'd been too poor to buy a second car, another reason she'd been walking that fateful day.

Angus dropped to his knees beside the antique chest, struck down by the painful memories. Deep sobs escaped his old body. He wept bitterly for Marigold and the time that had been robbed from them. He remembered Arty and Momma doing what they could to comfort him. But it had been Pearl who'd made him meals, took him dancing, and eventually breathed some life back into him. Pearl had deserved better than him, he realized. He hoped someday she'd find someone who could give her all the love and affection he couldn't.

After some time passed, Angus dried his eyes and stood to his feet. He closed the chest and pushed it further into the corner. He picked up the book and tucked it under his arm, then shoved the now tear-stained pages of the article and Marigold's grocery list into his pants pocket.

Descending the ladder from the attic, he whistled to himself. After setting the book on the dining room table, he started a fire in the fireplace, emptying his pockets and tossing their contents into the flames. Angus stared blankly into the hearth as the licks of amber consumed the reality he couldn't bear to face.

He wandered to the kitchen and rummaged through the drawers and cupboards until he found a blank sheet of paper and a pen. He sat down at the dining room table, next to the book, and wrote a note to his beautiful Marigold. He took the note, folded it in half, and pressed it between the yellowed pages of the book, in place of the grocery list she'd written for their picnic and the article he wished he'd never found. Suddenly very tired, he held the book to his chest as he wandered to the bedroom and laid down in bed atop the covers.

"I love you, my precious Marigold," he whispered aloud.

He thought he heard her whisper back as he drifted off to dream.

CHAPTER ELEVEN

*W*hen Pearl arrived back at home, the smell of rotting fish assaulted her nostrils before she reached the front porch. She noticed an overturned bucket by the steps, remnants of fish tails sticking out from the pail. Sidestepping the stinky mess and rolling her eyes at her husband's forgetfulness, she climbed the steps of the porch. She stood before the front door for a few moments to collect her wits about her, then knocked three times.

She wasn't sure why she was knocking at the door of her own home, but the months she'd spent away seemed like years. Not to mention Angus hadn't returned her calls the past two days and she wasn't sure where they stood. Their last phone call had been civil, pleasant even, but she still couldn't shake the feeling something had been off.

She knocked once more, then tried the door handle. The door was locked. Stretching her neck and shoulders to relieve the building tension, Pearl bent down and retrieved the spare key from beneath the flowerpot. She frowned, realizing the neglected, wilted flowers were beyond reviving. She turned the key in the lock and slowly opened the door.

The inside of the house was a disaster. Dishes were piled high in the sink, flies circling the untouched food that stuck to the dirty plates. Tools and scraps of wood lined the countertops. It looked as if Angus had started several home projects, only to get distracted and move onto something else. He'd always been a bit messy, but never a slob.

When she rounded the corner to the family room, she was shocked by the countless bushels of silk, yellow and orange marigolds strewn across the coffee table and sofa. Several paint cans sat half-opened in the corner. Her stomach turned in knots. She'd known something wasn't right and she realized she should have come sooner.

She called out to Angus, her voice coming out in a high-pitched squeal. Her heart pounded as she headed down the hallway towards the bedroom she had shared with Angus for so many years.

"Angus," she called once more. The bedroom door was closed. She knocked on that door too, hoping for an answer.

When she opened the door and looked inside, she saw Angus sleeping peacefully atop the covers. Sighing with relief, she crept to the bed. Her husband appeared to be smiling. He had a book clutched to his chest. She leaned down to shake him awake but stepped back when she felt the chill of his skin. She knew he was dead. She supposed she knew it the moment he hadn't answered the front door.

As carefully as she could, Pearl removed the book from his hands. *Pride and Prejudice*. She'd never known Angus to be a reader, let alone a romantic. She was about to place the book on the nightstand when a slip of paper fell out of it and landed on the quilted comforter. She set the book down and gingerly picked up the piece of paper.

The book was clearly old, but the paper looked new. She unfolded it, smoothing it out over the blankets. Then, slowly, she held it up and began to read it.

My darling wife,

I love you more than words could ever express. Though we've been apart for so long, I see your face each night when I close my eyes. I'm glad for the time we had together. Despite how things ended, I have no regrets. My heart is full and I will always love you.

Eternally yours,
Angus

Tears of contentment sprung into Pearl's gray-green eyes. Angus had died happy. Despite how he'd acted towards her in recent times, he'd died loving her. She could take comfort in his final words to her and move forward with her own happiness.

After the Climb

CHAPTER ONE

*T*he crew cab truck ascended the remote road at a crawl, the gravel crunching beneath the pickup's oversized tires. Leah felt her pulse quicken as she studied her pink nail polish and agonized over her situation. How could she have been so stupid? She'd been a teenager once. She knew what it meant when a boy asked a girl to take a drive out to the middle of nowhere. She also knew what Erik's expectations would be once they reached the top.

She'd grown quiet and her palms had begun to sweat but Erik didn't seem to notice. His voice was smooth and rich as he continued to talk in detail about growing up in his hometown. Back at the restaurant Leah had found his tone soothing, but now her heart raced as she searched for double meanings and innuendos behind his every word.

She wanted to ask him to turn the truck around, but she didn't want him to think she was a tease. At every twist and turn in the road, in her head she was screaming for him to go back. Back to the cozy diner booth they'd been sharing when he'd suggested coming up here;

and where she, for reasons that now escaped her, had jumped on the idea. But she didn't scream. Instead she sat silently beside him as the vehicle continued to climb.

When they reached the top, Erik put the truck in park and opened the sunroof. He leaned his head back against the cloth seat, closing his soft, brown eyes as he let the evening breeze tousle the dark waves of his hair. "Great, isn't it?" he asked, flashing her a grin, then turning his focus toward the rolling hills and city lights far below them. "I've always loved it up here."

The view was spectacular, but Leah was in no position to enjoy it. She remained silent, too frightened to speak. She liked him. Was even wildly attracted to him. But she wasn't the sort of girl who gave it up on the first date. She needed to take things slow. Especially after her previous relationship had been such a disaster. So why had she said *yes* when he'd offered to bring her up here? She knew why. Because there was something about him that made her trust him. And there was also something about him she'd found exciting—and she hadn't wanted the evening to end.

But now she feared she had spoiled everything. She was either about to turn him down, in which case he'd likely be angry at her for wasting his time; or she'd acquiesce to his desires, something she'd later resent him for through no real fault of his own. The lump in her throat had grown to the size of a grapefruit. It was suffocating. She clasped her hands together and placed them in her lap, silently scolding herself for allowing herself to get into this predicament.

"Ooh, I've got something for us," Erik said, penetrating the silence and her tormented thoughts. He didn't seem at all nervous.

Why should he be? He wasn't a teenager. He'd probably had lots of practice at this sort of thing. For reasons she couldn't explain, Leah's stomach turned at the thought of him bringing other women to the same spot.

He reached around to retrieve something from the floor of the backseat. She knew it was likely a box of condoms, or a cheap bottle of wine, and her eyes flickered to the door handle as she fought the urge to flee.

Whatever he retrieved from the backseat was concealed in a plastic grocery bag. He opened the bag and pulled out a packaged item from inside. When Leah's eyes adjusted to see what it was, her shoulders relaxed and she burst out laughing.

"Red Vines? You brought licorice?"

A faint dimple fluttered on his cheek. "Well, yeah, they're my favorite snack." He tore open the packaging with his brilliant white teeth, pulled out two vines, and handed her one. She accepted it, graciously, though she doubted she could swallow anything with the lump in her throat.

"I just hope now that you got me up here that you don't expect me to put out," Erik said, grinning widely and taking a generous bite out of the licorice.

When he shot her a wink, Leah grinned back at him as visible relief washed over her pretty face. The dread she'd been feeling moments earlier was replaced by overwhelming gratitude. Unable to stop herself, she threw her slender arms around his neck.

"Hey, hey," he teased, pretending to fend her off with the licorice in his hand. "I'm just here for the view, lady."

She laughed, then snuggled closer to him on the bench seat. When she rested her head on his shoulder, Erik kissed the top of her head. He breathed in the coconut scent of her honey-blonde hair but he didn't pursue anything further. To Leah's surprise, he seemed genuinely interested in the view—the smattering of lights from the town below mixed with the full moon and bright stars that lit up the night sky. It was truly breathtaking.

Leah inhaled deeply, drinking in the cool night air. Her earlier fears were banished far away. When Erik laced his fingers through hers, she felt completely at ease. At that moment, on a first date that could have ended in disaster, she realized she'd found the character of the man she wanted to spend the rest of her life with.

Savannah

CHAPTER ONE

*W*hen Savannah Logan made up her mind about something, that was it. There was no stopping her. And right now her mind was made up to get out of her car and give the driver in front of her a piece of her mind. She was familiar with the traffic light between 36th and Broadway. She had at least a minute to tell the man off—the man who, moments ago, had cut her off in traffic and she'd almost spilled her coffee on her newly purchased cream blouse. By her estimation she would only need thirty seconds to give him a good and proper tongue-lashing.

Savannah climbed out of her car and marched to the driver's side window of the black sedan. She tapped on the window, careful not to chip her polished nails, then placed her hands on her curvy hips.

"Bob, I'm going to have to call you back," Toran spoke into the phone when the unwelcome knocking on his window interrupted his conversation. He put down the phone, then rolled his window down, slowly. "May I help you?" He was polite, but his face didn't mask his annoyance.

"Yes," Savannah told him. "Yes, you can help me. You can help me by paying attention in traffic and not cutting me off so we can both reach our destinations safely." Her blue eyes flashed and her cheeks warmed with anger.

Toran studied her shapely figure and refined facial features. As he did, his gaze was cool. Collected. She was cute, he decided. Not exceedingly beautiful, but attractive enough to make a man stand up and take notice. "My apologies," he said evenly. "I was on an important call. If I cut you off, it was not my intention."

"Well, perhaps if you stayed off your phone and kept your eyes on the road, it would help matters." She turned on her heel and marched back to her car, keenly aware that she'd let her temper get the better of her, and even more painfully aware that the stranger she'd just bawled out was possibly the most attractive man she'd ever laid eyes on.

When Toran arrived at work, he couldn't get the hot-tempered brunette out of his mind. In hindsight, he should have gotten her number, but, he reasoned, she hadn't been in the mood to give it out. He couldn't shake the feeling she might be the one that got away.

He usually didn't talk on his cellphone when he drove, but he was neck deep in bringing a merger to close and the call had been crucial. He should have pulled over he reckoned, something he now regretted. But not as much as he regretted not catching the name of the fascinating, incensed brunette who had chastised him without mercy right there in downtown traffic. He'd been impressed. He was used to people kissing up to him versus staring him down. Okay, he was more than impressed; he was a little bit smitten.

CHAPTER TWO

*W*hen Toran ran into Savannah at the food trucks only two days later, the chance encounter took him by surprise. Taking advantage of a rare break between meetings, he'd walked down the street to grab a hotdog. Savannah was strolling down the sidewalk, licking ice cream from a waffle cone. Toran thought she looked almost delicate doing so. But based on their brief encounter on the road, he knew *delicate* was far from the appropriate word for such a woman.

She came to a dead stop when she saw him. He strode over to her, all confidence and swagger. "I'm not distracted by my phone now," he told her.

She wanted to smack the smug grin from his face; but more aggravating than that, she wanted to kiss his gorgeous lips. When she stared into his green eyes, she found herself softening. "Probably not my finest moment," she admitted, biting her lower lip. Her eyes held a glint of an apology, but the fire that had caught his attention days earlier still burned.

"No worries," he said. "I was in the wrong. I'm Toran." He extended his hand towards her.

After transferring her cone to her left hand, she shook his hand, pleased his handshake was firm. She was also pleased his gaze was on her face and not on her chest. She'd been full chested since fifteen, a fact most boys—and now men—recognized immediately and didn't bother to hide their admiration for.

"Savannah," she said.

"You work around here, Savannah?"

She nodded towards the office buildings. "Building C. Eighth floor."

"No kidding?" he chuckled. "I'm building B. Eleventh floor." A drop of ice cream ran down her cone and dropped on her blouse. Instinctively, and without hesitation, Toran reached over to wipe it away. His fingertips unintentionally grazed the swell of her breasts. He could feel the lacy bra beneath the sheer material; feel her body respond to his touch.

Savannah took a step backwards. "Excuse me," she said in protest as she tried to bring her heartrate back to normal.

Toran made no apologies. He licked the drop of ice cream from his fingertip, savored the familiar strawberry flavor, then returned his focus to her. "Have dinner with me tonight."

She put her hands on her hips and pursed her lips. "Is that a question?"

"No." he said, stepping closer to her. He lowered his voice. It was both commanding and soothing. "I'd very much like to take you to dinner, Savannah." He searched her eyes for an answer.

"Fine," she said, giving in for reasons she couldn't fathom. "I get off at six. I'll meet you here and we can decide where to go."

He watched as she sauntered away. He'd changed his mind. She wasn't just cute. She was the most beautiful, fascinating creature he'd ever met.

After an exhausting workday, Savannah rode the elevator down to the main floor, hoping she didn't look as drained as she felt. She ran a small, women's support organization and between the long hours and heartbreaking stories she was barraged with daily, some days she felt like she had nothing left in the tank.

Toran was waiting for her in the lobby, looking refreshed and smug. She stood up straighter. So much for meeting at the neutral territory of the food trucks. She smiled and waved, suppressing the urge to slug the handsome face that wore no hint of weariness from a long workday.

"Your place or mine?" he asked.

This time she did slug him. Square in the shoulder.

"Ouch, I'm kidding, I'm kidding," he said, chuckling as he held up his arms in surrender. "Where would you like to eat? And please don't say the food trucks."

Laughing, Savannah said, "There's a great pub and brew off sixth avenue. It's actually within walking distance." She wasn't sure why she offered up her favorite place to unwind. If the date went badly, she certainly didn't want to have to find a new restaurant to avoid running into him again. But something told her this date was going to be anything but disappointing.

Toran nodded. "Sounds great." A beer and a burger girl. He wouldn't have pegged her as such. If she also liked baseball, he reckoned she may very well be *the one*.

When they entered the pub, the sign read 'Seat Yourselves' and Savannah didn't hesitate as she grabbed a handful of peanuts from the bar, then made her way to a booth with a perfect view of the T.V. Toran's favorite baseball team was playing and he celebrated a little on the inside.

"You like baseball?" he asked, taking a seat opposite her.

"Hate it," she said, grinning and shooting him a wink as she popped a shelled peanut into her mouth.

Toran freed himself from his tie and placed it on the seat beside him.

"So, tell me what you do, Toran," Savannah said, taking in his obviously expensive and custom-tailored suit. His wardrobe was a far cry from the tasteful yet inexpensive thrift rack purchases her non-profit organization salary allowed.

He picked up a menu, worried this date was going to turn to small talk, something he didn't prefer. "I'm a lawyer at Thomas and Reddick," he said as he read through the menu. "We specialize in mergers and acquisitions."

"So, you're sort of a shark." Toran glanced up sharply but was relieved to see she wasn't glowering or frowning at him. Her words were simply matter of fact.

"I've been accused of it a time or two." He laughed, hoping it wasn't inappropriate to do so. It wasn't yet clear how she felt about his livelihood.

"I'll bet they've already made you partner," she said smoothly.

He nodded, trying to appear humble.

"Good," she said, opening her menu. "Then you can afford to buy me dinner." And with a wink and a smile, she steered the conversation to more important matters, baseball, capturing his heart in the process.

Savannah and Toran inhaled dinner, skipped dessert, then scurried back to the parking garage to retrieve their cars. They were like two teenagers anxious for a roll in the sheets. "Your place or mine?" Toran asked again, but this time it wasn't in jest.

"Yours," Savannah said without hesitation. She was dying to see if his homelife was as polished and perfect as the outside image he presented.

He hoped the cleaning lady didn't flake out on him. "I can drive us," he offered.

Any other man, she would have turned him down, flat. She liked to be in control, and riding with him limited her options of walking out whenever she felt like it. Then again, any other man she wouldn't be rushing back to his place after only one date. What was wrong with her?

Sensing her hesitation, he said, "Or, you can just follow me."

She frowned, considering. "I'll ride with you," she said, giving in. "But you're driving me back here later. I don't do overnights."

"Fair enough," he said, pretending to give in. He didn't usually do overnights either. But he also wasn't about to let this one go.

CHAPTER THREE

Two months in and Savannah was spending more time at Toran's than she was at her own place. She'd taken over his top dresser drawer and more than half his closet space. The pair had settled into a routine of going on an early morning run, then cooking breakfast together before carpooling to their separate offices. Their lives merged seamlessly—friends and family blending without incident.

On one end of the relationship, that wasn't a surprise. Savannah had little in the way of family or friends; always keeping herself at arm's length from people. But Toran had an army of both. Savannah was hesitant to integrate with a new crowd, but she took a liking to everyone Toran introduced her to. Like his taste in suits, she decided, he had excellent taste in those he allowed to get close to him.

They sometimes fought, as two passionate people will do. But it was always a fair sparring match. No berating; nothing below the belt. During one such fight, the worst thing he'd called her was *challenging*. It was more of a compliment than an insult she realized. Afterwards he'd teased her that she was more of a formidable opponent during an argument than any lawyer he'd gone head to head with.

They always made love after a spat. It was important to both of them. Tonight had been one such occasion. They'd argued over something silly. The pros and cons of rent control, if she recalled correctly. One minute their voices were raised and the next they were tearing off each other's clothes and headed towards the bedroom. When it was over, they laid tangled in each other's arms, their bodies slick with exertion. Savannah rested her head on Toran's chest as he stroked her hair.

"I love you, you know," he said quietly, surprising the both of them. Those were three words he didn't throw around lightly—especially after only dating someone for such a short time. And he certainly never said them if he didn't already know what the response would be.

Savannah lifted her head and rested her cheek in her palm, contemplating her next move. She loved him too, of that she was certain. But should she tell him? With those words came certain expectations. Expectations about commitment and a future. She had decided a long time ago she'd never marry. Would it be fair to tell him she loved him if she didn't plan to stay?

"You don't have to answer just yet," Toran said with a laugh, unfazed by her lack of response. He tucked a strand of her hair behind her ear and kissed the tip of her nose. "Take your time."

"I love you too," she admitted aloud. She had never been more at ease around another person—a fact that was starting to terrify her. As Toran drifted off to sleep, content with her response, Savannah wrestled with her next move.

Savannah was unusually quiet over breakfast the next morning as she mulled over her relationship with Toran. She'd need to end it, of course. She was starting to depend on him, and she had no room for that. If her parents had taught her anything, it was that relationships rarely ended in happiness. She'd end things tonight. She'd already worked it out in her head. Tonight, over dinner, she'd drop the bomb. It would be better in the end, she reasoned. For both of them.

CHAPTER FOUR

"You've been quiet all day," Toran observed as they left the restaurant and walked towards the parking garage. It was late and the streets were almost empty.

Savannah shrugged her slender shoulders, not sure how to respond. She had chickened out over dinner and her window of opportunity to end things before the evening was over was closing fast. They'd driven into work together, something she now regretted. It meant she would have to endure the long car ride back to his place after she revealed it was over. From there she would pack her things and make the lonely drive back to her apartment.

She wrestled with her earlier decision. How could she possibly tell him it was over? He was the most incredible thing that had ever happened to her. And he'd given her no reason to end things—other than that she'd grown to rely on him. That was reason enough, she reminded herself. She needed no one. That was the way she preferred things.

"Baby, what's wrong?" He stopped and turned to face her.

She'd never let anyone else call her *baby*. Out of someone else's mouth it sounded cheap and condescending. But she liked the term of endearment when it came from him. It always sent a pleasurable chill down her spine.

When she still refused to look him in the eye, Toran tipped her chin upward with his fingertips. "Savannah?"

She met his gaze but her eyes flickered with apprehension. "I think we should take a break," she blurted out, needing to retreat from him but unable, or unwilling, to let him go completely.

He blinked back at her but didn't respond. His handsome face was a mask.

She prattled on, nervously. "We've been going full throttle, and I just think it's time to pump the breaks a bit."

He continued to stare at her, considering her words as he watched a thousand emotions flicker across her pretty face. Then his eyes narrowed and he spoke. A single word. "No."

"Excuse me?" She straightened her shoulders and prepared for a fight.

"I said, no." His tone was firm. Dispassionate.

Savannah was shocked into silence.

"You're scared," he said. "This is what you do. Things get a little uncomfortable and you run. Well not this time. I'm saying, no." As he spoke, he glowered at her, burning a hole through her soul.

For an eternity of seconds, she glared back. Then, unable to help herself, she softened. "I knew you wouldn't make it easy for me," she whispered, smiling faintly.

He stepped towards her, confident and unrattled. "Oh, I can make some things easy." He placed his firm, capable hands on her curvy hips and reveled in the involuntary shudder his touch prompted in her. She was everything he'd ever wanted, and even if she refused to admit it, he knew she felt the same.

"Marry me, Savannah," he said, his eyes trained on hers. "I love you, and I'm not going anywhere." Then he pressed her to him, parting his lips and closing the conversation as his mouth claimed hers.

After the Thaw

CHAPTER ONE

$\mathcal{R}$achel Jacobs slid that month's alimony check and neatly completed deposit slip across the granite countertop to the bank teller. *What pushes a man to the point where he'd rather pay a woman not to be part of his life?* she wondered. Tears stung her eyes and threatened to escape down her cheeks as she thought of how her once beloved Timothy now preferred to cut her a monthly check to stay away rather than welcome her back into his home. *Their home.* Hadn't she been a good wife? Eighteen plus years she had been a faithful companion to him. Dinner was always prompt. The house, immaculate. Perhaps she'd tried to be too perfect. The magazine image she'd worked so hard to project might have felt cold to Tim. *Stifling,* he'd asserted towards the bitter end.

"Will that be all ma'am?"

Snapping back to the present, Rachel said, "Yes, thank you." She smiled sweetly at the young teller. The smile was genuine, but it failed to reach her solemn, green eyes. She trudged out of the lobby and back to the aging car Tim had *generously* let her keep. Once behind the wheel, she leaned forward in the worn leather seat, her auburn hair falling over her face, and let the bitter tears flow.

Married at eighteen with a baby on the way, there was a time she thought she and Tim had everything going for them. Now, with little Lacy off to college, at thirty-seven the pair realized they'd grown apart. Or that is, Tim realized it for them.

"We have nothing in common except for our love for Lacy," he'd admitted over the prime rib dinner she'd worked so hard to prepare.

As much as she'd wanted to argue, the truth he'd spoken had landed hard and settled heavily in the pit of her stomach. She had always depended on Tim for support, especially with the finances. She had been content making a home for their family of three. But now, with Lacy gone, along with Tim's love, the thought of depending on him for her everything felt wrong. It made her feel weak and insignificant.

The monthly spousal support was generous, her husband's lawyer friends had explained. Funny how at one time she had considered them her friends too. Another misjudgment in the life she'd thought she'd built. At first, she had vowed not to take the monthly payout. She had some savings squirreled away, including a modest inheritance from her great-aunt.

But two months on her own and no job prospects in sight, Rachel had depleted her savings and was forced to rely on the money her ex- provided. Few places were looking to hire a woman approaching forty, with only a high school education and no job experience save for her volunteer work with the PTA and local soup kitchen.

When she'd moved out, she'd secured a small, two-bedroom house four blocks down from her previous home. Sometimes she drove by her old house, the one she had shared with Tim and Lacy for so many years. But last week when she'd driven by in the late evening and saw a second car in the drive, she'd vowed to never go back.

She'd recognized the car. It belonged to Emory, a slim, beautiful lawyer from Tim's firm. Rachel's tears had fallen hot and bitter as she'd made her way back to the lonely two-bedroom house she couldn't yet bring herself to call home. She'd long suspected Tim had feelings for Emory. There were the text messages, the late-night phone calls—all masked under the guise of work. Tim had dismissed her suspicions in the past.

"How could I think about someone like that, when I have someone like you?" he'd ask, then he would kiss her cheek and go back to pouring over case briefs.

CHAPTER TWO

*H*ealing a shattered heart and crippled pride takes time. The healing is slow at first. Almost nonexistent. Then, one day you realize the soul-crushing heartache you've been carrying around has been reduced to a dull ache that is almost tolerable.

For Rachel, it took a solid six months to get to that point, but she considered it a great victory once she did. With a long but satisfying workday behind her, she smiled to herself as she turned the key in the front door lock, realizing several hours had gone by without a single thought of Tim.

Her cellphone rang as she was making her way to the kitchen. She set her purse on the countertop and let her cell go to voicemail. The ping a few moments later announced she had a new message. She would get it later, she reasoned. Right now she wanted to enjoy a hot bath and a glass of wine. It was her way of celebrating the small wins in her long journey of healing and self-fulfillment. Her therapist, had she bothered to obtain one, would be proud.

The second glass of red wine went down smoother than the first. When Rachel was with Timothy, she hadn't even been aware you could purchase wine for only six dollars a bottle. Her husband had been a bit of a wine snob, making her one by default. In her months alone she'd learned to be more frugal with her purchases. Tonight she had splurged on a ten-dollar bottle, which, disappointingly, hadn't tasted much better than a six-dollar bottle. But after she'd consumed, admittedly chugged, her first glass, her taste buds were desensitized to the offensive taste. Now she could appreciate the bitter bursts of flavor that came through as the second glass went straight to her head.

She thought about work and it made her smile. Her boss, Jane, had taken a chance on her. Jane was a bit of a man-hater and when Rachel had explained in the interview why she was starting a career so much later in life than most, Jane had offered her the administrative assistant job on the spot. On Rachel's first day, some of the other administrators warned her about her new boss—noting she could be a tyrant. But Rachel and Jane worked well together, and only a few short months later, Jane increased her responsibilities and was dropping hints about promotional opportunities.

Rachel's bathwater had turned cold and her skin was pruning. Reluctantly, she drained the tub and stood to retrieve a towel from the towel rack. She dried herself, then stepped out of the tub, wrapping the towel tightly around her. She considered checking her voicemail, but instead opted to brush her teeth and call it an early night.

CHAPTER THREE

$\mathcal{W}$illiam Conrad finished leaving a brief message, then tucked his cellphone back into his shirt pocket and returned his focus to studying the plans he'd drafted for a new parking garage downtown. It wasn't his most imaginative work, but he had logged some killer hours to design it and he knew his clients would be pleased.

"You still trying to score a date with Rachel on the fourth floor, Billy?" Larry, his co-worker and oldest friend, teased.

William's handsome face split into a wide grin, but he didn't answer. Since the moment he'd first laid eyes on Rachel, he couldn't get her out of his thoughts. She worked as an administrative assistant, just two floors up from him, but often came down to deliver blueprints or get his signature on outgoing design schematics. Each time he saw her, he offered to take her out for coffee, but each time Rachel politely refused him.

"It's never going to happen, y'know," Larry continued. "She's too frigid."

The smile faded. "Don't call her that. You don't know anything about her."

"Um, neither do you."

"I know enough about her to know there's more to her than what she's willing to let everybody see."

Larry shook his head in disbelief. *Smitten* was the word he would use if asked to describe how William felt about Rachel. *Disinterested* was what he believed Rachel felt in return. But there was no arguing when his old pal had his mind made up about something. And right now William's mind was made up that underneath Rachel's cool, stony exterior was a woman worth pursuing.

CHAPTER FOUR

$\mathcal{R}$achel stirred the cereal in her bowl as she replayed last night's voicemail for the third time.

Hi, Billy here. Um, from the architecture floor. Listen, since you seem to have something against coffee, I thought … what about if I take you out to dinner instead? Anyways, if you're free tomorrow night, say, around seven, I'd love to take you out. Think about it, okay?

She smiled to herself, then saved the message, though she'd already committed it to memory. She should find his persistence displeasing. Inappropriate, even. The cynical part of her did. But the small part of her heart that hadn't frozen solid over the past months found it endearing. William seemed sincere. Despite what she'd heard about him, he didn't make her feel like a prize to be won, then discarded, but rather someone worthy to be cherished.

Mind made up, Rachel dialed his number. With her heart pounding in her chest, she politely accepted his invitation to dinner.

"But let's make it seven-thirty," she said. The change in time was for no other reason than to retain some semblance of control.

Despite the fluttering in her stomach, Rachel appeared poised when she walked through the door of the restaurant wearing a black dress with a flirty hemline that was catching the eye of anyone within striking distance with a pulse. Her auburn hair, instead of being pulled tight into its usual, professional updo, hung loose around her shoulders. William stood to his feet, leaned over to whisper something to the hostess, then smiled and waved Rachel over.

"Your table is ready," the hostess announced once Rachel reached the podium. "Right this way, Mr. Conrad." The hostess was openly gawking at William, clearly taken by his tall, athletic build and confident presence, but he kept his eyes trained on his date.

"I can't believe you were able to score a same-day reservation," Rachel marveled as she fell into step beside him.

"I made the reservation two weeks ago," he admitted.

A gentle laugh escaped her perfectly glossed lips. "You were that sure of yourself, were you?"

This time it was William's turn to marvel. Rachel's laugh brightened her face, making her more beautiful than he thought possible. Her green eyes, usually so sad, danced with humor. It tugged at his heartstrings. "Hopeful, at least," he admitted with a shrug. "Of course, I did have to do a little peddling to get the reservation slid from seven to seven-thirty." His eyes narrowed in playful jest.

Feeling a twinge of guilt, Rachel started to apologize, but thought better of it. She didn't want to lose the upper hand she was trying so hard to keep. "I'm afraid it couldn't be avoided," she said instead, keeping her tone light but William noticed her cool demeanor return.

Once they were seated, Rachel hid her nerves behind the oversized menu.

"What do you like here, William," she asked, enunciating his name as if addressing someone in a high court.

"Please, call me Billy."

"What's good here, Billy?" she asked, lowering the menu below her chin and smiling again. It was a ghost of a smile, but he took it as a positive sign. From what he'd seen, she rarely smiled at work, at least not one that wasn't forced.

"I like the prime rib, but I hear the salmon's fantastic."

"Hmm," she considered. "I'll order the rack of lamb then."

William studied her. To the untrained eye, she appeared impassive, but he noticed the smile that tugged at the corners of her mouth, threatening to escape.

He chuckled. "You like to be in control, I see."

"Does that bother you?" She rose one eyebrow.

"I think it's sexy as hell," he admitted.

Rachel's cheeks warmed at the unexpected compliment and she rewarded his statement with a smile that reached her eyes and brightened the room. Then, as quickly as it had come, the smile disappeared. "What's your play here, William?"

"Billy," he reminded her.

"What's your play here, Billy?" She set down the menu, lined it up perfectly with the corner of the table, and stared coolly in his direction.

He stared back at her, his blue eyes unblinking. "I'm not quite sure what you mean." He was unfazed by her accusing gaze.

"Oh, I think you do."

"Listen," he said. "I like you. You intrigue me. I think somebody hurt you badly, and you're afraid to open up. But underneath all that polish and poise, I think there's a woman who is warm, caring, and sexier than advertised. I'm interested in getting to know *that* woman."

"Well," she said, taking a sip of her water. He noticed her hand shook slightly though her voice remained controlled. "I'm afraid you're going to find me disappointing."

"I don't believe that for a minute," he told her.

The waiter appeared to take their orders, then whisked away the menus when he left. William was glad to be rid of the paper shield he could tell Rachel was desperate to continue hiding behind.

"Tell me something about yourself," she said after a few moments of silence passed between them.

"Well, I'm the youngest of three brothers. I've been an architect with the firm for going on ten years now." She nodded, urging him to continue. "I don't have any kids. I've never been married, though I came close to popping the question once." He paused, staring intently into her eyes. "And I don't give up on something once I know what I want." He resisted the urge to reach across the table and take her by the hand.

Her gaze flickered to her water glass, then back to his. "Really?" she challenged, her confident air returning. "Go on."

"And I don't scare easily," he finished. His blue eyes were soft and warm as he held her hard, cool gaze.

Despite her attempts to remain controlled, Rachel found her resolve softening. Her shoulders relaxed and before long she let her guard down and fell into casual conversation. Each time she pressed her hand to her lips to stifle a giggle or leaned conspiratorially across the table to divulge a minor yet not-too-personal detail from her past, William basked in the small victories. She was like a beautiful flower, opening its petals for the first time.

"You intrigue me, William," she confessed when the evening was drawing to a close and they were standing on the street corner, each waiting for a cab.

"Billy," he corrected again, still patient.

"Billy. I'm glad I accepted your invitation to dinner."

Her cab rolled up to the curb. He took her by the hand and pressed it to his lips. She didn't jerk her hand away, but instead let it linger in his. "It has been my sincere pleasure," he told her. And he meant it. She was more than he imagined, and all that he desired. He was beyond smitten in a lustful, passionate sort of way. He was head-over-heels in love. A first for him.

CHAPTER FIVE

William wanted to tell Larry about his date the night before, but he didn't want his comments to get back to Rachel and for her to think he had been bragging. Gossip traveled fast in the six-story office building. Instead, he kept details of the evening to himself, which is why Larry was even more surprised than William when Rachel sauntered through the glass doors of the architectural suite that morning and made a beeline to the drafting table where the two men were standing.

"Good morning, Billy. Larry," she offered pleasantly. She wore her hair down once again and had traded her typical slacks and sensible flats for a tasteful pencil skirt and kitten heels. William gawked. Larry gawked harder.

"Good morning to you," Larry said while William was still searching for his words.

"Hi," William finally managed, finding his voice again.

"Listen," Rachel said, looking only at William and biting her lower lip. A subtle blush crept across her porcelain cheeks and her nimble fingers fidgeted with the drafting pencils on the desk as she fought to regain her faltering confidence. "Does your offer to grab coffee still stand?"

He smiled back at her. "Absolutely."

"Good. Want to come grab me in about an hour or so?"

William nodded. Larry stood, open-mouthed, watching the scene unfold.

"Perfect. See you in a bit." Then, as quickly as she'd come, she was gone, leaving both men speechless.

"What just happened?" Larry teased once she was out of earshot.

Chuckling and shrugging his shoulders, William said, "I told you she'd come around."

"I wouldn't celebrate yet. It's taken you months to get her to agree to coffee. Typically you'd have a woman on her back, then discarded by the end of a work week."

William frowned. He knew he had been a rogue all these years, using women as he saw fit. Truth being told, they were using him too. It was a mutual understanding. But Rachel was different. Despite what Larry believed, he wasn't interested because she was a challenge, though he did enjoy the chase. He genuinely cared about her.

"Earth to Billy."

"She's the one, Larry."

"I'm not going to lie," his friend admitted, "I'm starting to see the appeal."

William nodded, finding amusement in the way Rachel had arranged the drafting pencils in a neat row before making her exit. He thought he understood her; her need to control what she could in a world that seemed to be spinning out of control.

"I was beginning to think you didn't like coffee," William teased as they stood in line at the coffee stand on the rooftop of the building.

"Nah, it's just that coffee's such a personal experience."

He stole a glance at her. "I'm not sure what you mean."

"I find I can tell a lot about a person by the type of coffee they order."

"Really?" he looked skeptical.

"Really. There are certain coffee orders where I know immediately, it would never work out between us."

"Next, please," the barista called.

William stepped to the counter, studying the menu for the appropriate drink to order. Now he was nervous. He typically liked black coffee. None of this fancy, highfalutin stuff. But perhaps that would make him appear boring.

"What can I get you?" the barista asked, smiling, but she used a tone that suggested he should consider placing an order sometime that month.

"Um, well how about you go first?" he told Rachel.

She started to laugh and her eyes twinkled with humor. "William."

"Yes?"

"I'm messing with you. Coffee is coffee. Order whatever you want."

He chuckled, but she could see the relief on his face. "Black coffee, no cream, no sugar," he said. Then he looked over at Rachel and shot her a wink. "Make it extra bold."

"I asked around about you," Rachel said once she and William were seated at a small table with their coffees.

His eyes flickered nervously to hers, then back to his drink. "And?" he said calmly, though calm was far from what he felt. He wondered if she was messing with him again.

"And ... it turns out you have somewhat of a reputation." This time when his eyes met hers, she wasn't smiling and he saw the pain behind them she wasn't bothering to mask.

"If I told you you've changed me, would you say it was just a line?" He kept his tone playful, but he studied her expression.

She smiled back at him. The sadness in her eyes vanished, replaced by curiosity and ... dare he hope ... desire. "I think people can change," she finally answered. "At least, I hope they can."

Without thinking, William reached across the table and stroked her cheek. Her skin was warm and soft. She didn't retreat. She kept her eyes level with his. Eyes locked on each other, the passionate heat they exchanged was hotter than the scorching coffee they were pretending to drink.

For the second time that day, William was lost for words. *I've never met anyone quite like you. You're what I look forward to every day.* He feared everything he desired to say would sound like a line to Rachel, and she was far too good for anything but honesty.

Instead, it was Rachel who spoke. "I want to see you again, Billy," she said. They were just the right words.

"I would like that very much."

"Good. Meet me downstairs after work? Say, five?"

He nodded. He had a meeting at five. He would need to move it. When they stood to leave, he noticed she had rearranged the coffee creamers into a neat stack and separated the sugar packets from the sugar substitute.

She looked down, then flushed. "Habits," she explained, her tone apologetic.

Williams eyes crinkled with humor. "You fascinate me," he said.

CHAPTER SIX

*T*o the amazement of both of them, William convinced Rachel to come to his place for dinner. She knew she should refuse. She needed to take things slow and being in someone's home with easy access to a shower and a bed was a surefire way to *not* take thing slow. William had seen the hesitation in her eyes the moment he had asked, but to her credit, she'd accepted his invitation with grace. They walked to the corner market, picking up a few groceries, before sharing a cab ride to his apartment.

"This place is amazing," Rachel said, taking in the views from his high-rise apartment building. *How can anyone afford to live here?* was the question she wanted to ask.

"Perks of helping design this place," William explained, though Rachel sensed there was likely more to the story.

She went to the window and stared down at the waterfront and parkway below. "It's beautiful."

"You're beautiful," he said, coming up behind her. He'd startled her. He could see it in the way her shoulders shook, but she didn't turn around.

Take it slow, he reminded himself.

Rachel turned to face him. When she spoke again, her tone was cold and formal. "What is your plan for the evening?"

William was not deterred by her indifference. He knew it was a shield. "Dinner. A little wine by the fireplace. Then I'm sending you packing. I have to get in early tomorrow."

His words set her at ease and her lips curved into a timid smile. "Alright. That all sounds good." Nervously, her eyes flickered toward the bedroom. The door was partly ajar and she could make out the inviting, king-sized bed. She was pleased to note it had been neatly made.

William strode to his bedroom door, shut it, then grinned at her. "No expectations," he told her. But his groin tightened thinking about having her in that room. For a moment he imagined how she would feel; how she would taste as her auburn hair fell across his chest. Larry had been right. Most women William showed interest in would have already shared that bed with him long ago.

"Wine?" he asked, reining in the lustful thoughts he hoped weren't scribed across his face. When she nodded, he crossed the room to the liquor cabinet, retrieved a bottle of Cabernet Sauvignon and a bottle opener, then poured two glasses. He filled his glass generously. Not wanting to give her the wrong idea, her portion was more modest.

Seeking courage, Rachel drained her glass more quickly than she'd intended. She smiled shyly as she held it out for a refill.

William laughed, taking the glass from her and filling it more liberally this time.

"Can I help with dinner?" she asked, steering them towards his kitchen where the groceries still waited on the countertop.

"You're just dying to put everything away, aren't you?" William teased. "You like everything to be in its place."

The wounded look in her eyes showed he had hit a nerve. "Suffocating, right?" she asked, her ex-husband's devastating words ringing in her ears.

William stepped toward her. Wordlessly, he took the glass from her hand and set it on the counter. He smoothed the hair out of her face with his strong hands. "Intoxicating," he said.

He lowered his lips to hers, slowly, giving her a chance to refuse him. When she didn't, he lengthened the kiss. Her lips were full and warm and he drank greedily. To his everlasting pleasure, Rachel returned the kiss with equal fervor. Her arms went around his neck, pulling him closer as she stood on her tiptoes to meet his mouth. When he finally stepped back to give her some air, her eyes shone with passion.

"I like you for exactly who you are. Never feel like you have to change anything."

After one more, soft kiss, William tore himself away and began to prep dinner. Rachel worked to return her breathing to normal and marveled at the feelings William stirred inside her. Feelings she thought had died but instead had been lying dormant for longer than she cared to admit. Far before Tim had asked for a divorce.

"Dinner was delicious," she said, looking around at their empty plates and glasses but, surprisingly, not feeling any need to remove herself from the comfort of William's couch to load them into the dishwasher. She tried to recall the last time a man made a meal for her. Never, she supposed. Tim had made it clear from the beginning that the kitchen was her place in the household, not his.

"What's wrong?" William asked, seeing the expression on Rachel's face shift from content to soured.

"Oh, nothing, sorry. Just thinking." She smiled up at him, then bravely rested her head on his broad shoulder. The wine had made her a bit sleepy.

He lifted a tendril of her auburn hair, twirling it around his fingertips. "You can stay over if you'd like," he said softly.

Rachel jerked upright. Adrenaline coursed through her as her eyes darted around the apartment for wherever she'd kicked off her shoes.

"Hey, relax, Rach. I didn't mean anything by it. I just saw you were tired, and it's getting late. I can sleep on the couch."

Her shoulders relaxed a bit, but she still had a wild look in her eyes. "No, I must really be going. Thank you, William," she said as she stood to go. All formalities had returned.

"Rachel," he said calmly. When she didn't answer, he stood and faced her. "Rachel," he repeated.

This time she looked at him. The hurt in her eyes was unmistakable. "I'm sorry he hurt you," he said. "But I'm not him."

Rachel stared at him, blinking back tears. Then, wordlessly, she reached for her shoes and headed for the door. William stayed put, his feet glued to the floor, and watched as she walked out of his apartment, hoping it wasn't for good.

When Rachel called the next day, it surprised him.

"I hope you're not upset about last night," she said.

"Why would I be? I had a great time." His heart pounded in his chest. He was surprised by the reactions she incited in him.

"Can I get a do-over?" she asked after a pause.

William chuckled. It was a deep, throaty laugh and Rachel smiled from the other end of the line. "Does this mean I have to cook again?" he teased.

"Nope, this time I'll bring the food to you. Hope you like Chinese take-out."

"Take-out sounds fantastic."

When they had polished off dinner, Rachel stood from the couch to gather up the empty food containers. "You can leave 'em," William offered.

"You should at least know me better than that," she said, but she was smiling.

"Fine, be the one to change my slobby, bachelor ways," he teased, but he pulled her back onto the couch and onto his lap. She squealed with delight and rewarded him with a chaste kiss on the cheek. He pushed back the hair from her face and kissed her properly. Rachel closed her eyes and allowed herself to get swept away by his warm mouth and masculine scent.

"I want you, Rachel," he confessed, then tensed as he waited for her response. He knew he had agreed to take it slow.

To his surprise, she whispered back, "I want you too, Billy."

A growl escaped his throat as he crushed his lips down on hers. Rachel felt her own stirring within. She could not recall having wanted anything so badly. Her body ached for him to hold her. For him to fill her. Fighting for the control she knew she needed to surrender, she allowed him to help her up from the couch. Her heart slammed in her chest but she let her hand rest in his as he led her to the bedroom.

Rachel stopped inches from the bed. When William leaned down to kiss her, he caught the hesitation in her eyes.

"We don't have to do this," he told her. "No expectations." His taut manhood was throbbing in protest, but his words were sincere.

"I want this, Billy," she whispered.

"You sure?"

"Don't make me beg," she teased, though her eyes misted. "You know I like to be in control."

"I think I'd like to see the begging," he admitted with a devilish grin as he cradled her face in his hands.

His hands slid to her hips as he once again crushed his lips against hers. In a frenzy, they reached for each other, fumbling with buttons and zippers in a half-crazed attempt to come together, skin against skin, and squelch the fires that burned between them.

They fell into bed. Rachel moaned when William jerked her panties past her hips and kissed the apex of her thighs. She arched towards him, un-shy and deliciously out of control of her emotions. "Oh Billy, please, please," she begged as his tongue waged its gentle assault and she pleaded for him to end her suffering. He kicked out of his jeans and covered her body with his, careful not to crush her as he eased inside.

"Yes, oh Billy yes," she screamed.

Frigid she was not. She was hot and smooth and wet. She opened herself up to him without coaxing.

"Damn, you're lovely," William moaned as he sank inside her. He didn't hold back. Couldn't hold back. He was a man possessed. He had intended to be gentle but she propelled him into madness and he drove harder and harder inside her. With each thrust she left him dizzy, but she begged him to continue. Demanded it, really.

She arched her hips toward him, matching his rhythm as she lost herself in him. "More," she demanded, no longer caring that she had relinquished control of her emotions. "Oh, Billy, please more."

His heart was slamming in his chest and he concentrated on not climaxing as he took her higher and higher. He could tell she was getting close and he growled with desire as his mouth claimed her throat.

She moaned as she tightened around him, then found her release. She would be his undoing and his lips covered hers as they reached their climax. "Rachel, Rachel," he murmured over and over as he felt the soft spasms of her womanhood surrounding his swollen rod.

William knew Rachel had changed him, but it wasn't until that moment that he realized how much. The William of his past would have scrambled out of bed to grab a quick shower and avoid the awkward silence that often came after lovemaking. His leaving the bed would make it clear the relationship would not carry beyond sexual desires—and would reaffirm the rule he'd typically make clear prior to taking things to this level: there were to be no overnight guests.

Instead he slowly rolled to his side, keeping Rachel cradled in his arms. He wrapped one leg protectively around her and kissed her hair. "Stay with me?" he asked.

Rachel didn't tense beside him. She lay perfectly relaxed and content. "Mmm...," she responded, and he took it as a *yes*.

"You fascinate me, Rachel. I promise I'll never take you for granted."

"Mmm...," she murmured once more, before contentedly drifting off to dream in the arms of the man she now knew she loved.

CHAPTER SEVEN

"*L*et's go to my place tonight," Rachel suggested over the afternoon coffee that had now become part of her and William's daily work routine.

"Really? You ready for that?" He looked at her in admiration and surprise. Somehow her willingness to let him see her place seemed like the biggest step they had made in their relationship that had gone from budding to blossoming in a short amount of time.

"I'm ready," she said. "Be prepared for color-coordinated sock drawers and a kitchen pantry with all the food labels facing outward." She laughed as she said it, but William could see the nervousness in her eyes and knew she worried he would judge her harshly.

He grinned instead. "I do love that about you, you know."

She smiled at his unexpected comment, eyes glistening with tears of happiness. "You don't mind my crazy?" she challenged.

"I love you and your so-called crazy," he told her. And he meant it. Once thinking himself incapable of love, he now loved absolutely everything about her.

She set her coffee cup down and stared over at him. "I love you too, you know," she confessed aloud for the first time.

"I know."

"Did not!" she laughed.

He gave her a smug grin. "I knew before you realized it. It was just a matter of time."

"Oh really," she was giggling, the carefree laugh he loved and knew was always there beneath the surface.

"I mean, I'm told I'm pretty irresistible." He winked at her.

"Well, you are that." She leaned across the table and rewarded him with a quick peck on the cheek. She didn't look around to see if anyone had witnessed their exchange. She no longer cared.

Rachel thought she would be nervous as she and William shared a cab to her two-bedroom house. It wasn't as grandiose as his apartment, but she was proud of the life she had been building there. Proud of the life she knew was hers. She no longer relied on alimony checks to get by. It had given her great pleasure the first time she'd mailed one back. She had sold her car, always preferring walking and public transportation anyway. With the money from the sale of her car, and a little bit of overtime funds, the house was now furnished and decorated to her taste.

When she unlocked the front door and opened it to invite William in, Rachel smiled broadly. She didn't feel nervous. She felt completely at peace, because for the first time since she had moved there, she knew she'd finally come home.

Once Upon a Book

CHAPTER ONE

Cassidy Chambers stood staring out the windows of her third story hotel room, surveying the beach below. Children laughed and played happily on the swings, their parents pushing them back and forth to the point of exhaustion. Young couples strolled down the beach, hand in hand. An old man wrestled with a kite, trying his best to tame the wind into submission.

Cassidy exhaled slowly, then took another swig of the bitter hotel coffee. When she'd arrived at Seaside almost a month prior, she never thought she would tire of the ocean view that lined the picture windows of her suite; the rolling waves, the sun setting over the water. Her agent had gone through a lot of trouble, and expense, to book the place for her on such short notice. But now she was bored. Bored and restless.

She knew things didn't hold her attention for long. She was like a spoiled child with a newfangled toy; attracted to the new and shiny. But after a time, the toy was discarded. That was Cassidy's approach to many things in her life. Enjoy for a time, then discard.

The image of her boyfriend—now ex-boyfriend—Scott, popped into her mind. There had been an immediate attraction when they had first met at one of her book signings. All physical, of course. He had been tall and lean and gorgeous. More into himself than her (if she recalled correctly, he'd only been in the bookstore that day to purchase some sort of muscle magazine), but she hadn't minded. At least not at first. But after a time, the newness wore off and she found herself wanting. Wanting more than the pretty picture the two of them presented to the outside world. Two young, attractive people in a relationship that didn't run any deeper than Scott's flawless, bronzed skin.

Cassidy turned her attention back to the windows. She noticed a man in his late twenties walking down the boardwalk. He was a handsome man, but that's not what drew her attention. He had a book in his hand and was headed towards one of the benches outside the hotel. She strained her eyes to see what he was reading, but she wasn't able to make out the title or the author.

Curiosity piqued, she scooted the wingback chair closer to the windows and took a seat. The man sat on the bench directly below her. He leaned back, legs casually crossed at the ankles, and began to read. He didn't pull out his phone or use his book as a cover to gawk at the young women who jogged by in their tight yoga pants. He appeared truly engrossed in the novel, only glancing up from time to time to peer out at the ocean.

Cassidy smiled to herself. A man who enjoyed reading and solitude were two traits she greatly admired. As he read, she studied him. He was above average height, but not towering. He had good muscle definition. His build suggested he obtained his muscles through hard work and general activeness as opposed to spending hours at the gym. His sandy blonde hair was cut short in the back but left a bit longer on top. She liked the way the wind tussled it about.

A curly haired little girl came bounding down the walkway and tripped, skinning her knee. Her mother was several feet behind her, looking exhausted as she pushed a double stroller with two more kids in it. The handsome man set down his book, coverside up, and rushed to the little girl. He helped her up, then extended his hand to shake that of the little girl's mother. Still frazzled looking, but smiling (probably a bit smitten), the mother shook his hand before setting off down the path with her three children.

After waving goodbye to the little girl, the man strolled back to his bench. Still curious what he was reading, Cassidy quickly stood from her chair, took out her phone, used the zoom function of the camera, and took a snapshot of the book cover. The camera flashed against the windowpanes, taking her by surprise. At that moment, the man looked up towards her. She stepped back from the window. Had he seen her? Surely not, she reasoned. She had to believe the hotel windows were tinted from the outside, and she was, she reminded herself, three floors up.

Writing it off as a coincidence, Cassidy took a seat once more to examine the photograph she'd taken. The picture was blurry, but she could make out the author's name and half the book title. She searched on both in her internet browser, and the book came up in the results.

With bated breath, she clicked on the link. She didn't know why she was so nervous. Perhaps she worried she'd be disappointed with his book choice. But disappointed she was not. It was an autobiography written by a world-renowned female scientist who documented her journey from a poor girl with wild theories to a successful, respected member in her field. Cassidy smiled. She loved stories about triumphs of the underdog.

Realizing she had probably been studying the man more than was normal, she stood from her chair, gazed one last time, then wandered to the kitchenette to warm up her coffee and get started on her day. She had overdue pages to write. She had promised her agent she'd finish the first draft of her latest project by month's end. Her agent was more than happy to arrange her hotel stay based on that promise. But now, nearly a month in, she'd hardly written a word. The ocean views didn't prove as inspiring as she'd hoped. But this morning, she was inspired to write. She took out her laptop and the words flowed as she thought about the handsome stranger below her.

You learn a lot about a person when they think no one's watching, she mused. Having observed him for only a few, fleeting moments, she knew more about him than she could derive from a month of dating him. He was kind to small children, appreciated nature and a good book, was rarely distracted by his phone, was comfortable enough with himself to be alone … and he had a glorious head of thick hair that he raked his fingers through when he was lost in concentration.

When Cassidy looked up at the clock, she was surprised to find it was past two in the afternoon. Her stomach growled, reminding her she had skipped lunch. She looked down at her word count on her laptop. She had managed about 8,000 words and figured her agent and editor would be happy about the progress. At this pace, she could finish the first draft by the end of the week.

She closed her laptop and wandered to the kitchenette to get something to eat. Finding nothing appetizing in the fridge, she decided to try out the fish taco truck she'd seen on the street corner. She grabbed her windbreaker, then strolled out of her room, opting for the stairwell over the elevator.

Starved at this point, she was pleased to find the food truck line was sparse. She was studying the menu when she heard a voice from behind her.

"Have you eaten here before?"

She spun around to see who spoke. Her cheeks turned pink when she realized it was the mystery man with the book, but she mostly kept her cool. "No," she said, "but I've been admiring the truck for a few weeks and thought it was time to try the food."

"You like to admire things?" he asked. His handsome face held the slightest smirk and she blushed again, wondering if he had seen her earlier. She shook off the thought, convincing herself there was no way he could know she was the same woman, even if he had somehow noticed her staring from three floors up.

"What are you going to have?" she asked, steering the subject away from herself and back to the food.

"Something light. I'd like to save room for dinner tonight. Do you have plans?"

"Plans?" she repeated, taken off guard.

"Yeah, for dinner."

"No." She spoke slowly, unsure what he was getting at.

"I'm asking you out," he explained. "Would you like to have dinner with me tonight?"

Cassidy was used to being asked out, but the handsome stranger's unrelenting confidence had her off her game. "Dinner sounds nice," she said, with all the poise she could muster.

"Great, I'll meet you at *Stormy's Chowder House* up the street, say, seven?"

"Sounds great." She liked that he didn't try to impress her by suggesting one of the more posh restaurants. "I'm Cassidy," she said, extending her hand.

He took her hand in his. It was warm and firm. "I'm Kevin," he said. "It's a pleasure to meet you."

She was all nerves as she prepared for her date. She threw on a black and white polka dot dress she'd purchased at one of the local shops. She smoothed down the fabric, then brushed out her hair for the umpteenth time. Nervous wasn't her typical M.O. but something about the intriguing stranger, something about Kevin, had her reeling.

She reached the restaurant ten minutes early but Kevin was already seated at a booth near the back. He stood to wave her over. He had traded his shorts and t-shirt for casual slacks and a blue polo shirt. He looked gorgeous. Cassidy reached the booth, gave him a semi-awkward, exhilarating hug, then took a seat across from him.

Her nerves dissipated the longer they spoke. Kevin had a way of putting her completely at ease. She learned he owned his own construction company and was in Seaside to place some bids. He had four older siblings, had never been married, but was a proud uncle to six nieces and nephews.

Cassidy revealed she was an author and the reasons that brought her to Seaside. Hours passed quickly as they enjoyed the pan seared oysters and clam strips, but more than that, they enjoyed each other's company.

When the meal was almost over, Kevin said, "Oh, I forgot."

He reached beside him, produced a book from the bench seat, and tossed it casually on the table. Cassidy shot him a strange look when she realized it was the book he had been reading earlier.

"Just finished it today. It's yours if you want it."

She still stared at him, speechless.

"Well," he continued, "you seemed so intrigued by it earlier, I thought you'd like to read it." He shot her a wink and his lips curled into a devilish grin as his eyes gleamed in amusement.

She should have been embarrassed. She should have sunk to the floor beneath the booth. Instead, she burst out laughing. "I can't believe you saw me," she said, shaking her head.

"I can't believe I had to be the one to come find you after all of your gawking," he teased.

"You mean our meeting at the fish taco truck wasn't by chance?"

"Nah," he chuckled. "All part of the plan." He sat back, casually studying her. "I have another confession."

She sat up straighter, intrigued. "Really? What's that."

"I've seen you around for a week. Been waiting for the right time to talk to you."

"Really?" Cassidy's voice came out in a higher pitched squeak than she'd intended. She sounded like a teenager with a crush. Well, she had the crush part right.

"Yep," he continued. "You usually like to take walks on the beach in the morning. Today I went down there, thinking you would come, but you didn't."

"I see," she said, baffled. "And how do you know this about me?"

He grinned, mischievously. "We're in the same hotel. I've been watching you from the fourth floor."

She burst out laughing again, then stood, leaned across the booth, and kissed his luscious lips. "Is the view better one floor higher?" she whispered.

"It is from where I'm standing."

They left the restaurant, hands intertwined. Cassidy smiled to herself, realizing Kevin was someone she would never tire of. He gave her hand a tight squeeze, feeling exactly the same.

Double Rainbow

FOR CODY

I cried when I heard you were gone, and the skies cried too.

Then I saw a double rainbow and it made me think of you.

I called out your name, as I chased it down the street.

It remained in view but just out of reach.

I stopped to stare at the colorful arches, tracing across the sky.

You see, I saw you in that rainbow, and suddenly I realized why.

Your family is that first rainbow, a reflection after the rain.

As we reflect upon your memory and stand strong against our pain.

That second rainbow is beautiful but somewhat faded from our view.

But if we look up, it's still right above us.

That second rainbow is you.

Sherree's Song

A TRIBUTE

You loved like you lived—unwavering and bold

You had a passion for people and a heart of gold

You were dedicated to your horses, your family, and friends

You loved beadwork, country music, and roping the wind

No matter what life threw your way, you didn't let it keep you down

You were always laughing; we rarely saw you frown

Yes, we sometimes argued, as loved ones will do

And at times we hid from yet another family photo, this much is true

When you were here, the holidays seemed brighter

If I'd known that hug was our last, I would have held on tighter

With every visit you brought baked goods and a smile,

As you waltzed into our homes in your unique western style

Now you're gone, and our hearts refuse to heal

There's a hole in our lives no one else can fill

Why did you have to go? Only God and the angels know

We rejoice you no longer suffer, though our tears, they still flow

The world was more beautiful when we had you to share,

But heaven is more beautiful now that you're there.

Where Hearts Are Mended

CHAPTER ONE

𝓑ethany Davis stared out at the lake, trying her best to swallow the lump that formed in her throat whenever she thought about Todd. Todd, her beloved husband of eleven years, who had breezed out of her life as unexpectedly as he'd wandered into it.

They had met by chance during college. They were from different campuses but had both attended the same seminar on criminal behavior. She'd gone to the speaking engagement for the much-needed extra credit to pass her Advanced Psychology class. Todd had attended out of pure interest—planning to pursue a degree, then a career, in criminal law. Charming, but of average looks and build, Todd had managed to capture Bethany's attention, not by his appearance, but with the intelligent questions he'd launched at the speaker and the witty retorts he'd fired at the immature hecklers in the back of the venue.

She'd asked him out for coffee afterwards; something that was out of character for her. She'd been shy back then but also hadn't been willing to let him slip away. He'd later revealed if she hadn't asked him out, he'd planned to ask her instead.

They dated for under a year before tying the knot. Too little time in the minds of their family and friends, but neither Todd nor Bethany could be talked out of the union. When they renewed their vows on their ten-year anniversary, those same family and friends toasted to their good fortune.

But it hadn't all been a bed of roses. The pair had loved each other, absolutely. But along the way Todd had also developed a love for the drink. On some occasions, that love had proven stronger than they were. He'd come home late, stumbling into the house with whiskey on his breath.

He was never a mean drunk, that much Bethany was grateful for. If anything, he was more carefree. The stress of his caseload often had him on edge, but when he drank, the frown lines of worry disappeared. When he'd come home in a drunken stupor, she'd always be waiting up for him. He'd ignore her worried protests, twirling her around in the living room and telling her she was the most beautiful thing in his world. But his love of spirits led to drinking at the office, eventually resulting in the loss of his job.

Not long after he was stripped of his career and dignity; and following a bitter fight in which he'd refused her pleas for him to quit, Todd went off drinking. Alone. He had attempted to drive home drunk, something he'd promised her he'd never do. Sometimes he would call a cab, or she'd pick him up; or he'd sleep it off at a friend's house nearby. But on that fateful night, he'd gotten behind the wheel and wrapped his car around a telephone pole. Nobody else was hurt, the state patrolmen told her when they delivered the news to her doorstep in the middle of the night. Bethany knew she should have been relieved by that fact. Instead, she was angry. Perhaps she wanted someone else to suffer alongside her. Or maybe she wanted a reason to hate Todd for leaving her alone in such a cruel existence without him or the security of his love.

She had been struck down with grief and disbelief when she'd learned of his death. Openly, she had wept. But on the inside, she had cursed his name for leaving her alone in a now-empty world. Early on in their marriage he'd convinced her they didn't need to have children; that all they needed was each other. She hadn't considered what that would mean if tragedy tore them apart.

A bitter tear slid down Bethany's cheek and landed on her hand. She brushed it away, noticing her wedding ring for the first time. She hadn't been able to bring herself to remove it. Todd had slipped that ring on her finger on the day they were married and for more than a decade she hadn't taken it off. Today she glowered at it. Then, eyes filled with tears, she yanked it off and threw it into the lake. She watched as the golden circle with the diamond chip disappeared below the surface. On her wedding day the officiant had told her that circle represented eternity. What a farce eternity had turned out to be.

Once the ring disappeared from her view, she thought she'd feel guilty. Instead, all she felt was loneliness. "It's time to get over you," she said aloud to Todd. He didn't respond back. Then her shoulders began to shake as the cold reality sunk in that he never would.

CHAPTER TWO

"*T*his seat taken?"

The unfamiliar voice startled Bethany, and she looked up from her cup of coffee and empty plate of pie. She wanted to be annoyed, but the handsome, sandy-haired stranger who smiled at her with those warm, blue eyes made her want to smile back.

"It's all yours," she told him.

She was seated at the counter of Bonnie's Diner, a local hot spot in the town of Ardor. She'd happened upon the town and diner when she was passing through on her way from Charlotte, North Carolina to Memphis, Tennessee. She'd chosen Memphis because she didn't have any friends or family there. There wouldn't be any prying, sympathetic eyes whenever she walked into a room. No whispers of sympathy. Or judgement.

But as she drove through Ardor, she spotted a sign announcing *Fresh Peaches* and felt compelled to pull over. After purchasing a half-dozen, she sat down on the curb to consume her prized acquisition. As the juice from the peaches ran down her chin, she realized the delicious fruit only served to rouse her appetite. She drove a bit further into the sleepy town where she discovered the diner. She moseyed in, ordered lunch, and the rest was history. After only a few hours, she'd found no reason to leave; only reasons to stay—one of those reasons being the huckleberry pie she'd just polished off before the blue-eyed stranger interrupted her private thoughts.

"Passing through?" she found herself asking. She probably sounded like a local. She was a local now, she supposed. She'd been living in Ardor for almost six months now, though she still lived out of a suitcase and had several unpacked boxes in her small, one-car garage.

"Actually, I'm moving here. Just bought the place," he admitted. "I'm Mac. Mac Parsons."

When he extended his hand to hers, Bethany took it hesitantly.

"Bethany," she said, offering only her first name. "You bought this place?"

"Yes, ma'am."

"But you don't know what's good here?" Her eyes narrowed in suspicion. She hoped he hadn't purchased it for the property, only to tear it down and build a condominium or pave over it and make it into a parking lot. She had a vested interest in the place remaining open.

He laughed. "I know what *I* think is good here," he explained. "I was just curious to know what *you* thought was good here. It dang sure ain't the coffee."

This time it was Bethany's turn to laugh. He was right, of course. The coffee was terrible. The delicious huckleberry pie made it almost tolerable, but even the pie wasn't enough to cover the bitterness of the sludgy brew.

"Sort of tastes like burnt dish soap," she admitted.

When he nodded in agreement, she asked, "What made you buy this place?" She was still hoping he planned to keep the diner open and prayed she wasn't devastated by his response.

"I just needed a change in scenery. I discovered this diner when I stopped in on my way to a business meeting. Fell in love with the pie and the people. I asked around, heard the owner had an interest in selling, and decided I needed to make sure the place stayed open."

Bethany studied him, wondering with suspicion if there was more to his story. She decided he was at least mostly telling the truth. She had also heard the previous owner had been interested in selling. Thomas, the restaurant manager, had once filled her in on the diner's backstory. Apparently, a town legend named Bonnie kicked her *no-good, cheating husband* out and opened the diner with the funds she received in the divorce settlement. She ran the place for as long as she was able, and her daughter after that. After both passed away, with no remaining children or siblings, the diner was left to a distant relative named Henry who lived in New York. By default Thomas was promoted from assistant restaurant manager to manager. Henry let Thomas run the place, gladly accepted the net profits deposited into his account at the end of each month, and to the relief of the entire town, stayed out of their business while the diner remained open.

But lately Henry had been calling Thomas regularly, prying deeper into how the business was doing and whether real estate was going up. On one such occasion, the owner finally revealed to Thomas his plans to put the restaurant up for sale. Thomas had offered to buy it on a monthly payment option, but Henry wanted the entire sum. Cash.

"Do you do things like that often?" she finally asked.

"Like what?"

"Buy restaurants on a whim."

"God, no. My financial advisor would have my head. He's always the first to tell me the restaurant business is a risky venture."

Bethany grinned. "Sound advice." One of the wait staff walked by, offering to give her coffee a warm-up, which she politely declined.

"My parents recently passed," Mac said, unsure why he was revealing so much to a complete stranger. "They left me enough money to where I could quit the job I hated. But I also knew I'd go crazy sitting around. I was on my way to a job interview in a big city with a big, fancy firm. And something just didn't feel right. Then I found this place…"

Bethany gazed at him, awestruck. It was exactly how she'd felt about Ardor. Something about its small-town vibe and charming residents had beckoned her to stay.

"Must sound crazy, right?" he asked, noticing her dumbfounded look.

"Not at all. I was just thinking about how much I can relate."

He grinned at her. "So you didn't grow up around here? Almost everyone I've met, seems like they've been *born and bred* here."

"Nope. I'm a new recruit as of about six months ago." She smiled as she spoke, but there was sadness in her eyes Mac could tell she fought to cover up.

"Well, good, then I won't be the only newbie. Hope you'll still come back to this place, despite the coffee."

Break over, Bethany pushed back from the counter, revealing her yellow and white gingham uniform and white apron. "I will as long as the new owner doesn't fire me," she said. Then she shot him a wink and sauntered behind the counter and into the kitchen, leaving Mac speechless.

CHAPTER THREE

*I*n a small town, it didn't take long for word to spread about the new, handsome owner of Bonnie's Diner. With the news came a myriad of things people wanted to know. *Would he change the name of the diner? What were his qualifications to run a restaurant? Would he change out the staff? Was he single?* That last one was Bethany's personal favorite, and admittedly, a question she wouldn't mind knowing the answer to.

She was also nervous about his plans for the restaurant. Mac had already assured her the pie would stay—but what about the employees? He had held an all-staff meeting two days prior to announce his plans for the place. Bethany, who'd been called back to Charlotte to sign final papers on the closing of the house she'd shared with her late husband, had been unable to attend the meeting. With the house officially sold, she was relieved to close the final page in that chapter of her life, but it also meant being left off the work schedule and out of the loop. With questions about her future employment weighing heavily on her mind, she left her house earlier than necessary to start her midday shift.

When she arrived at the diner, Thomas was seated in a corner booth with Mac sitting opposite him. The two men appeared to be pouring over paperwork. She grabbed her apron off its hook, tied it in the back, then started towards the kitchen. Changing her mind, she headed towards the two men instead, her curiosity getting the better of her.

"Can I get you two gentlemen anything?" she asked, eyeing the papers.

"We're good," Thomas spoke sharply. His harsh tone was out of character for him, but she let it slide. She knew Thomas had had his heart set on owning the restaurant some day and it pained her that, at least for now, it would be a dream unfulfilled for him.

"I'll take a cup of coffee," Mac said, flashing her a conspiratorial grin. "I've heard a lot about it."

Bethany blushed. "Coffee, got it." She patted Thomas on the shoulder, letting him know all was forgiven, then made a beeline to the back counter to retrieve the awful coffee before the lunch rush started. She noticed the fancy coffee grinder and change in coffee brand right away. "When did this happen?" she asked aloud.

"This morning. And that's not the only change," Elsa, the diner's most gossiping waitress, spoke up. "There's a new dishwasher coming in."

"What do you mean? He hired a new dish washer? What about Louis?"

"No," Elsa corrected. "Dishwasher. As in a fancy commercial one. It's on order. Comes in Sunday."

Bethany's heart dropped. She knew Louis had been washing dishes at the restaurant for over twenty years. He was an icon at the diner and practically family to anyone who worked there. What would happen to him?

"So, does Louis know?" she asked slowly.

"Oh, heavens yes," Elsa said cheerily. "He helped pick it out. Mac promoted Louis to assistant manager since no one has held that position since Thomas got himself promoted. Gave Louis a big fat raise and two weeks paid vacation a year. Louis and Mac have all sorts of plans for making the kitchen run more efficiently. It's driving Thomas absolutely crazy, though he's pretty happy that he'll get paid vacation too." She sniffed, likely put out that she hadn't been offered a vacation package.

Two things surprised Bethany—one pleasantly, and one not quite so much. She was pleasantly surprised by the generosity the owner was showering on the staff. But she was unimpressed that Elsa, always the town flirt, was already on a first-name basis with him. It annoyed her although she knew she had no business letting it.

"Sounds like Mac is going to make some great changes," she said. She too could join this little charade of being on a first-name basis with the owner.

"Order up," Bethany heard the call from the kitchen. She scurried to the counter, gathering up plates of burgers, fried fish, and French dip sandwiches—all served with a generous heaping of sweet potato fries. It was a busy lunch crowd. Busier than usual. She suspected the town's curiosity over the new owner was the reason for the uptick in business. She concentrated on ensuring her tables ran smoothly, but inside she was a bundle of nerves.

Midway through her shift, Thomas mentioned to her that Mac wanted to speak with her once her shift was over. Considering how well the owner was treating Thomas and Louis, she told herself she had no reason to be nervous. But her internal pep talk hadn't helped and the closer she got to the end of her shift, the more she convinced herself he was going to let her go. Perhaps he took offense that she missed the all-hands meeting, though she hoped Thomas had explained her absence. Or maybe he'd been annoyed by her curious prying at the start of her shift.

"Am I fired?" she blurted out when she reached the booth in the back that Mac occupied.

"Why? Did you steal from the till?" he teased

Her shoulders relaxed a bit and she slid into the booth across from him. "No, I just heard you wanted to speak to me, and I guess my imagination got the better of me."

He chuckled. "No, no. I actually wanted to speak to you so I could apologize. I didn't realize you worked here when I was being so cavalier about being the new owner of this place. It was my intent to break the news to the staff in more of an organized fashion so I could alleviate any fears of layoffs."

Bethany felt relief, of course, but she also felt a stab of regret at the casual way he lumped her in with the rest of his employees when he referred to her as *the staff.*

Mac saw the look of disappointment the moment it flickered across her pretty face. He wasn't sure what caused her disappointment; only that he wanted to vanquish it. "Have I said something to offend you?" he asked politely.

"No. No, of course not. With the generous way you've treated Louis, I'd say you're going to be a fine boss, Mr. ... umm .... Mr. ..." She trailed off, unable to recall his last name and hoping he would fill in the blank.

"Mac," he said.

"Mr. Mac," she said, lips curling into a mischievous grin.

Chuckling he said, "No, just Mac. Please."

She smiled back at him, happy to report, to no one in particular (well, maybe Elsa if it came up) that she and the new owner were now officially on a first-name basis.

CHAPTER FOUR

*W*hen he'd first purchased the restaurant, Mac had plans to maintain a hands-off approach. From what he'd observed, the diner was already well managed. He wanted to make a few tweaks, to be sure; but Bonnie's Diner was a town staple and he didn't want to rile up the locals by making too many changes. Or risk pissing off Bethany, the spitfire waitress who offered her opinion so freely, whether he asked for it or not.

He'd been thinking of Bethany a great deal lately. Smart, beautiful. About five years his junior. Since he'd lost his wife eight years back, he'd been convinced there'd never be another woman who could catch his eye. That is until he'd seen her sitting in that diner, eyes closed in reverence as she'd savored her last bite of huckleberry pie. The sun had been shining through the windows that day, casting a beam of light where she sat. It was like the angels were sending him a sign and he'd felt compelled to go over and talk to her.

He wasn't sure what he'd expected as he'd strode over to her and asked if the seat next to her was taken. Whatever he'd expected, she had been so much more.

Realizing she worked at the diner had been both a shock and a godsend. He'd been pleased he'd get to see her again. As many times as she was on the schedule, really. It helped that she was a hard worker and the customers liked her. It would have been a bit awkward if she'd turned out to be an awful employee.

Mac rarely came to the diner when it wasn't Bethany's shift. For starters, there wasn't much need to if she wasn't around. Thomas was an excellent manager, and now that Thomas had come around to accepting Louis as his assistant manager, the pair made a formidable team.

Thomas hadn't quite warmed up to Mac yet, but he was starting to thaw. As owner, Mac didn't take it personally. He knew Thomas probably worried he was checking up on him anytime he came into the restaurant. He'd probably have to clue his restaurant manager in on the truth about his frequent visits if he wanted him to fully come around. That might get a bit embarrassing, but for the sake of the diner, he figured he could swallow some pride. Perhaps Thomas would value his honesty and offer some insights about Bethany. Mac brightened at the thought, then dismissed it, not comfortable with prying into Bethany's private life even if it was solely to get to know her better.

Whenever he came into the diner, Bethany was friendly but a little on edge. She acted shy around him. It seemed out of character based on how she treated the other customers. She also seemed to take a special interest in whatever he ordered to drink. Depending on the time of day, that included orange juice, black coffee, a cola, or the freshly brewed sweet tea he knew drew in so many customers.

"Would you like anything stronger in that orange juice?" she'd asked him one morning. "Louis doubles as a mean bartender and he keeps his drinks flowing strong."

She'd smiled as she asked, but Mac couldn't shake the feeling it was a test. He had, of course, politely declined. He didn't drink. Hadn't touched a drop since the night his wife and infant son were killed by a drunk driver on an evening trip to the grocery store. He figured the baby had needed formula or diapers. He'd been working late, as he often did in those days. Otherwise, he probably would have been the one driving to the store and they would have been tucked safely in bed at home. All these years later he still blamed himself despite the advice and stark protests from his sister and the therapist he saw for a brief time.

Bethany found herself looking forward to her shifts more than usual. The prospect of seeing Mac at work, parked there in the corner booth he'd claimed for himself. His presence brightened her mood. They often talked when the restaurant was slow. Even flirted casually. But he never asked her out. She was reasonably certain he was interested. But something seemed to be holding him back.

When she found out about his late wife and son, her heart broke for him. He hadn't told her, of course. Louis had let it slip somehow. She now understood Mac's lack of drinking. They had more in common than either of them had realized. Perhaps their loss was what had unknowingly drawn them to each other. Regardless of what attracted her to him, Bethany was now besotted. She reasoned if Mac didn't soon make a move, she was going to make one first.

CHAPTER FIVE

"*H*ello?" Bethany answered the phone beside her nightstand, roused from a pleasant dream.

"You awake?" Mac's pleasant voice came through the phoneline.

She shot up in bed, now fully awake. "I am now," she laughed. "What's up? Did you need me to cover a shift?"

"No, in fact, what time is your next shift?"

"Not until this afternoon." She racked her brain, trying to figure out why he would call.

"Perfect. Are you familiar with Cici's Bed & Breakfast?"

"I know *of* it. But it closed down not long after I came to town. Illness in the family or something. Why?"

"Can you meet me there in about an hour?"

Bethany glanced over at her alarm clock. 6:35 a.m. "You want me to meet you at Cici's? At 7:30 in the morning? At a place that's closed and is probably haunted by now?" She was teasing on that last part, of course. Sort of.

"Is that a problem?" Mac asked, laughing from the other end of the line.

"No, no problem. I'll bring my ghost spray." She hung up the phone, then sprang out of bed to grab a shower and get ready. She was anxious for whatever Mac had in store. Maybe this would be the day he'd finally stop beating around the bush and ask her out.

When she arrived outside the bed and breakfast, Mac's car was parked in the overgrown drive and she recognized a second car—that of Jeremy Tethers, the town realtor. Disappointed she and Mac wouldn't be alone, and more confused than ever about the purpose of their early meeting, she climbed out of her car and went inside. She found Mac and Jeremy standing in the front lobby. Jeremy had a measuring tape and a clipboard and was rattling off dimensions.

At seeing Bethany, Mac walked over and wrapped her in a hug. She felt warm all over.

"Thanks for coming," he said.

"Of course. Now do you want to clue me in as to what I'm doing here?"

"Well, I've been thinking about buying this place, and Jeremy here was filling me in on all of its potential."

"Wow, you're going to buy this place?" She looked around in awe. Despite being closed for the past six months, the place was in relatively decent shape. "What for?"

"To restore it, of course. I'd like to reopen it."

Her face lit up. "Oh, that would be lovely. It was a shame when it closed. Such a beautiful spot. I understand they also used to host weddings here." Her voice trailed off. She hoped she didn't sound too gushy.

"So you think I should do it?" He stared at her, raking his hands through his sandy hair and waiting for her response.

"You're asking my opinion?"

"Of course."

"Why?"

"Because you're a friend, you have a good head on your shoulders, and I highly value your opinion." When she didn't respond he said. "Besides, I can't recall you having a problem giving your opinion before."

Bethany laughed, despite being wounded by his *friend* comment, though she knew he meant it as a compliment. "Yeah, but this is different?"

"How so?"

"It's a huge financial decision. I don't know if I could handle the guilt if it didn't pan out."

"You let me worry about that," Mac chuckled. "Besides, if it doesn't work out, I'll just sell it and go on to do something different."

"Then, yes. Yes, I think you should buy it."

Mac turned to Jeremy. "You heard the lady. Let's draw up the paperwork." Then he kissed Bethany on the cheek, leaving her breathless, hopeful, and every bit as confused.

If Mac buying the diner was fodder for gossip, the rumor that he'd bought the abandoned bed and breakfast was positively newsworthy.

"Is it true?" Elsa asked Bethany when she showed up for her shift.

Bethany smiled, pleased Mac had filled her in on the news before the gossip broke. More importantly than that, he'd asked for her advice before moving forward with the purchase.

"Yep," she confirmed. "Mac needed more to do and thought restoring the bed and breakfast would be a good investment."

"You two sure have gotten close lately," Elsa noted, to which Bethany just smiled. It was true. She and Mac had been hanging out a great deal. The bond between them was unmistakable. But whether that bond stemmed beyond friendship was painfully unclear to her—and growing more painful each day.

CHAPTER SIX

The window between the lunch and dinner crowd was Bethany's favorite time of the day. She'd hang up her apron, Mac would pour her a cup of coffee from the kitchen, and they'd tuck away in their usual corner booth. They'd discuss the diner or Mac's plans for the bed and breakfast once all the permits were in order. Sometimes Mac would reach out to touch her hair or her cheek. But he never made a move beyond that. Bethany still clung to the day he'd wrapped her in a hug in the lobby at Cici's. His body had felt firm and he'd smelled of soap and aftershave.

"Can I ask you something?" she finally blurted out as they were tucked conspiratorially in the back corner.

Mac grinned, something he'd been doing a lot more lately. "Fire away."

"How do you feel about people dating at the diner?"

"I think it seems like a fine place to bring a date." His eyes crinkled in amusement. He knew that wasn't what she was asking, but he also didn't want to learn about whoever the man was who had managed to catch her eye.

Bethany flushed. "No, I mean…" She struggled to put her thoughts into words. "How do you feel about inner-diner romance?"

He rubbed his chin. This was his chance to discourage something he didn't think he could bear to watch. "I, of course wouldn't forbid it, but I don't think it's a good idea. If it ends badly, everybody suffers. And if everyone in the kitchen is miserable, you can bet that carries over to the customers."

His quick response was like a blow to her ego. She couldn't blame him if he wasn't interested in her, but she would have expected him to at least ponder the option of dating her; perhaps make excuses why two people at the diner should indeed give it a go. For reasons she couldn't fathom, tears formed in the corners of her eyes. She blinked them away, then said, "Well, with half the town working at your restaurant, and soon the bed and breakfast, you're really narrowing down your dating pool."

Mac laughed, his mood lifting when he realized she was throwing him into her inquiry. "Now, wait a minute, I didn't know that I was counting myself amongst the diner staff."

This was the opportunity, Bethany told herself, where she should sigh with relief, then ask him out. But instead she found herself defending his beliefs about not dating those you work with. "Now, you realize as owner, you run an even bigger risk if you date one of the staff. If things end badly, not only do the customers suffer, but it could hit you in the pocketbook too if the woman you date claims she feared she'd lose her job if she didn't agree to date you."

Mac frowned, considering her words. "Huh, well then you're right, that does narrow down my dating pool considerably, doesn't it?"

She nodded, disheartened.

"Spouses work together all the time," he reasoned.

"That's different. They're equal business partners. They both have the same vested interest in making it work."

He stroked his chin again, silent for a time. "Well, Bethany," he finally said, "in that case, you're fired."

She looked up sharply. "I beg your pardon?"

"No, that settles it. Since I can't date you while you work for me, I'm going to have to fire you. It's really my only option." By this time he was grinning and Bethany kicked him playfully from under the table.

His expression sobered and he reached across the table and took her hand in his. "But seriously, I enjoy our little chats and I'm interested in pursuing things further."

"Me too," she admitted. Her heart felt ready to leap out of her chest. "But I do need this job," she said, biting her lower lip and searching his eyes for an answer to their predicament.

"I have a solution, I think."

She smiled, relieved. "Let's hear it."

"Well, I'll be busy getting the bed and breakfast up and running. I could turn ownership of the diner over to Thomas."

Bethany sat up straighter in her chair. "Wow, you mean that? That has been Thomas's dream."

"I know. We've talked about it at length. He's drawn up several proposals to buy the diner from me, sort of a rent-to-own option since he doesn't have much capital, but I didn't think he or I were ready for that change. Until now."

Bethany's eyes shone with tears. She was happy it freed her up to date Mac, but so much more than that, she was happy she'd get to see one of her closest friends realize his lifelong dream.

"There is one other option," he spoke up.

She froze. "Would it still allow Thomas to buy the diner?" She didn't want to be responsible for her dear friend losing out on his dream.

"Of course. That's all but a done deal. My lawyers are drawing up the paperwork now."

She grinned at him, more impressed than ever, and that was saying something. "Okay, then what's the other option?"

"Thomas owns the restaurant. That's fine. But what if instead of you being my employee, we were business partners?"

"How can we be business partners if you're selling the restaurant?" She stared at him. He didn't respond—giving her time to draw her own conclusions. "Wait, you mean the bed and breakfast? You want to be business partners with me? Equal partners? In a bed and breakfast?"

Mac continued to say *yes* to each of her questions, loving the way her eyes shone brighter and cheeks turned pinker with each positive response.

She paused, considering. She couldn't be a waitress forever. And with the sale of her house she had quite a bit of equity to reinvest. She could help manage the place. She loved the idea of welcoming regulars on a first-name basis, floating from room to room, offering fresh towels; maybe putting those little mints on the pillows if the cleaning staff needed an extra hand.

"I do have some money set aside," she spoke up.

"There wouldn't be a need..."

"Now, hold on," she interrupted. "If we're going to be equal business partners, I'm going to put my equal share into the business."

"I bought the place for just shy of a million," he said bluntly.

Her eyes went wide, but she didn't miss a beat. "And when I say equal share," she said, grinning, "I mean I'll put in $200,000 and the rest will be sweat equity."

Mac burst out laughing, then held out his coffee cup in salute.

"To partnerships," Bethany said.

"To partnerships," Mac agreed, and both knew the new partnership they toasted went beyond a business arrangement.

CHAPTER SEVEN

The next two months were a flurry of sawdust, interior design decisions, and interviewing staff. Mac and Bethany bustled about the bed and breakfast, stealing longing glances and chaste kisses in the hallways but neither having enough time to take anything further.

While Mac was responsible for securing most of the financing, Bethany had proven herself to be a worthwhile business partner throughout the ordeal. Mac knew she'd be a hard worker; but beyond that, she brought her eye for design and a talent for fleshing out a good bargain. More than once she'd saved him thousands on labor contracts, remodeling costs, and décor expenses. Bethany was also skilled at reading people—sniffing out the hard, honest workers from the lazy or over-priced help. After a few hiring snafus of his own, Mac left all employment decisions to her.

Finally, on the night before their grand opening, with the last of the workers gone for the evening, the two had the place to themselves. The original wood flooring sparkled with the newly applied varnish. With new area rugs, a fresh coat of paint throughout, and the eclectic but pleasant pairing of rustic and new furniture, Cici's Bed & Breakfast had been restored to its former glory. Better than its former glory, in Mac's opinion. He and Bethany had made a great team—pouring their hearts, souls, and hard-earned money into making the place their own while still preserving its original small-town charm.

Not wanting to mess up any of the new furnishings, the pair sat down on the floor of the lobby with a pizza and a 2-liter bottle of cola. They touched their plastic cups of soda together in salute. Then Mac said, "I don't know about you, but I'm ready to burn this place to the ground if it prevents me from being near you for one more hour."

Bethany laughed, nearly spitting out her drink. She blushed down to her toes as she recalled all of the times she'd pictured making love to him in one of the many newly remodeled rooms. "I think I know where the chef keeps the matches," she offered.

Mac didn't skip a beat. He stood to his feet, pulled Bethany up and into his arms, and crushed his lips down on hers. There was an undeniable thirst between them; an inescapable heat that had been burning for months now without being quenched. Bethany moaned softly as Mac swept his tongue inside her mouth.

"What room should we christen tonight?" he teased as he nipped at her earlobe.

"Upstairs. Room eight. It's my favorite," she whispered back. Her body hummed with longing.

He chuckled, pleasurably surprised. He stepped back to gaze at her. "You *have* thought about this, haven't you?"

"Guilty," she said, unashamed.

"Oh, thank goodness. I thought I was the only one with impure thoughts."

They both laughed, their emotions a jumble of nerves and lust.

Mac said, "Funny, I preferred room twelve."

"Really?"

"No, kidding. I have no idea which room is which." The lust in his eyes was almost palpable.

"And you're going to help run the place?" Bethany placed her hands on her hips, pretending to be displeased with his inattention to detail when all she wanted to do was let him rip her clothes off and satisfy the craving she'd once thought she'd never experience again.

"Hey, I have other talents," he said, throwing up his hands and feigning offense.

Bethany flashed him a devilish grin. "Oh really? And what would those be?"

He pulled her close again and stroked her hair. "Guide me to room eight and I'll show you," he murmured.

"Have I ever told you that I admire your confidence?" she asked as she led him toward the nearest room, no longer interested in the number outside the door or what the inner décor might hold. When his firm body stretched out over hers, the satisfaction of knowing he wanted her as much as she wanted him were the only things that held any interest for her tonight.

As evening gave way to morning, Bethany and Mac lay tangled in each other's arms. They were content. More than that, they were blissfully happy—for they had both found the place where hearts are mended.

The End

Acknowledgements

I've been working on *Taken by Storm* since before I published my first book. I loved the characters but the story didn't feel like something I wanted to develop into a full-length novel. A friend suggested I write a collection of short stories instead. While at first short stories didn't appeal to me, once I started writing them, I became somewhat addicted and the stories and their characters took on a life of their own.

I'd like to extend an enormous *thank you* to my friends and family for continuing to be supportive in so many ways—from reading early versions of my books, offering input, coming to book signings, or just reaching out to ask about the progress of my current project or to provide words of encouragement.

And as always, to the readers—my continued, heartfelt thanks. It is an honor and a pleasure to share my stories with all of you. I sincerely hope you enjoy them.

About the Author

Blake Channels was born in Tri-Cities, Washington where she resides today with her husband and two children. She graduated from Washington State University and is a wife, mother, and finance professional by day and a writer in her heart and soul—and whenever her schedule allows. In addition to writing romance novels, Blake enjoys spending time with family and friends, soaking up the sun, camping, and curling up with a good book.

Books by Blake Channels

(In Order of Date Published)

♦ Darkened (Romantic Suspense)

♦ The Comforts (Sci-Fi Romance)

♦ Ash Fallen (Fantasy Romance)

♦ Taken by Storm (Collection of Love Stories)

Visit blakechannels.com to learn more about the author, read her blog, and stay informed about upcoming events and projects.

Made in the USA
Columbia, SC
10 May 2023

16369614R00159